CANDY HOLIDAYS

& OTHER SHORT FICTIONS

STAN LEVENTHAL

BANNED BOOKS   AUSTIN, TEXAS

A BANNED BOOKS FIRST EDITION
COPYRIGHT © 1991 by STAN LEVENTHAL

Published in the United States of America by Banned Books, Edward-William Publishing Company, Number 231, PO Box 33280, Austin, Texas 78764.

COVER PHOTO BY J.M. DALLESANDRO
COVER DESIGN BY ROLANDE R. BRITT

THANKS TO; CHARLES KERBS, KRIS LEWALLEN, MICHAEL E. O'CONNOR, JERRY ROSCO, SUSAN SANOFF BENJAMIN EAKIN, TOM HAYES, LATIFAH RABB, THE PUBLISHING TRIANGLE.

ISBN 0-934411-51-4

Leventhal, Stan, 1951-
    Candy holidays & other short fictions / by Stan Leventhal.
        p. cm.
    ISBN 0-934411-51-4 : $9.95
    1. Gay men—Fiction. I. Title. II. Title: Candy holidays and other short fictions.
PS3562.E8734C3 1991
813'.54—dc20   91-20320
                                                                CIP

This book is dedicated to

Michele Karlsberg

CONTENTS

OASIS MOTEL

Like a jungle beast peering through thick vines and broad leaves, he watched me as I arranged myself beneath the gray sky. I wanted to dye my winter-white skin a tawny brown. He wanted me to notice him but did not want to seem too obvious. The courtyard in the center of the motel allowed a rhomboid of sunlight to enter and illuminate the area surrounding the pool. I watched the man watching me. But like a shy animal he was reluctant to approach the pool with me beside it, an antelope who would wait until the other animals had finished drinking and departed before emerging into the clearing for a mouthful of cool water. I could have smiled at him, invited him over with words and gestures. But I pretended I did not notice him lurking behind the garden palms, closed my eyes and prayed that the clouds would dissipate, the sun come forth, my body grow warm, my skin glow.

He walked, furtively, to the other side of the courtyard and observed me from another angle. I shifted position—belly down, ass up—waiting for the sun to respond to my brain waves. A cool, sharp shock of wind descended into the courtyard; I shivered. Goosebumps appeared on my arms and legs. The sunny warmth that I associated with Southern California did not manifest itself that afternoon nor the two that followed. My perception of things—like cities, hotels and men—is usually all wrong. I think I know something but eventually find out that I am ignorant. My expectations are rarely met, my predictions usually inaccurate. Too often I'm swayed by the cleverness of the packaging and I find out too late that what's beneath the ornate paper and colorful ribbons is not quite what I wanted.

At one time the motel probably looked pretty swank, its vaguely Spanish exterior washed in bright pastel colors. But these had faded over the years. The greens, once lushly verdant, now appeared sickly. The pinks, soft and serene, had acquired a brownish tinge like rust. A movie queen who never resorts to face-lifts, breast implants or hair extensions, the motel was aging naturally, the former ingenue forced to play supporting parts like shrikes, harridans and bag ladies. Aside from a scrapbook of dated movie stills and yellowed newspaper clippings, the glory is gone. The walls, floors and ceiling of the Oasis might retain some memories, some remnants of the past that resonate on certain frequencies and wavelengths. But a casual glance reveals nothing of the former stature. Today it is old and worn and uninviting. Damp, musty odors have permanently settled into the cracks and old furnishings. Vapors, dank and aromatic, seem to rise from the mattresses, blankets and pillows.

I thought perhaps that I could nuke my skin, conduct my business and indulge in a bit of mindless pleasure. But all my calculations and projections were like leaves that fall from a tree, soon to die if not already gone.

What you see on the large screen—with the benefits of ocular technology—is not what you see holding a strip of celluloid to the light, handling it by the edge, trying to make out the tiny, vague image. A length of film is not a movie; a movie is not just a series of photographs. I couldn't tell at first what he looked like. Just a sense of human form and color, movement and motion, rustling in thick, tropical vegetation. As he moved about, beneath the catwalk, lurking in the shadows like a private dick in a B movie, I was able to discern eventually that he had coppery skin over a plump, well-upholstered armature, the thighs and upper arms bunched up like overstuffed cushions. Dark hair, a mustache. He was Hispanic or Latino. Whatever it is called these days that is not considered derogatory. I've heard people call them Chicano. I like the sound of that. I don't know if the guy was Mexican or Mexican-American. I didn't know his name at the time. I probably wouldn't even be thinking about him except that he was the last man I may have infected, the final chapter, perhaps, in the book of my sex life.

There was something very unusual about the young men who worked at the Oasis Motel. I couldn't figure it out exactly at first, but when I walked in, suitcase in hand, I noticed that the guy behind the desk seemed strange. His motions were very fluid, more feline than human. His eyes had a deep-set faraway look. There was a glistening, oily patina on his facial skin and his hair looked like it had been lathered with Crisco. He checked me in, gave me the room key and explained everything that I needed to know such as check-in policy for guests' visitors and where the ice-machine could be found. The next time I saw him he was wearing layers of red, pink and tan make-up, a large tiara clung to the top of a big red wig that dropped its metalic strands to the scooped, low cut of a clingy cobalt dress, the waist so slender I could have put my hands around it, with large breasts, like warrior melons, that seemed to move independently from the slim body they were lashed to, the whole package teetering on blue leather stilettos. He greeted me and smiled. Touched the silver and rhinestone pendant at his throat and sashayed past me. I took a sip of Jack Daniel's and watched his firm little buns punch the tight behind of the dress.

The man emerged from the jungle, lit a joint and moved to the far end of the pool, staring at me, inhaling deeply, sitting on a chaise. I looked up at the gray sky, searching for a break in the clouds, a schism in the smog. Then at the man, in black Speedos, folds of fat gathered at the waist, a surprisingly hard-looking chest, with arms like hams. His face

11

seemed sinister, untrusting, yet he stared at me with an intensity that suggested desire. I smiled, looked away quickly, shifted onto my back and closed my eyes.

All of my friends are terribly concerned with appearances. Aside from the fastidiousness of their sartorial decisions, their haircuts, muscles and apartment decoration, they are particularly, fiercely finicky when it comes to men. A man passes us on the street—I have to admit he's handsome—and my friends believe that we have been in the presence of a god. Certainly, the stranger's hair is boyishly insouciant, his face symmetrically interesting in its configuration of lines and surfaces, contours and planes, his body moves jauntily with his balls, behind, thighs and calves all filling the snug jean-space like customized ingots. He is sexy. He is handsome. He probably knows it too, which only partially accounts for my skepticism. Does he know how to suck a dick like a lollipop? Is he reassuring and a comfort in bed, saying the right words, smoothing out the wrinkles on the sheets of sexual sacrifice? Does he have a good sense of humor? Has he anything interesting to tell you? Does he think David Copperfield is a Dickens novel, a magician who does one television special per year, or has he never heard the name at all?

These things are just as important as the body-face considerations. Yet you can't know about these things just by looking. My friends seem to equate hot looks with good times. But I've fucked enough beauties to know that this is not always the case. Still, I'm reluctant to tell my friends that I'm attracted to a guy who falls very short of their rigidly elevated standards. They would not approve of the hairy jungle beast stalking me at a sex motel in Los Angeles.

In my rented room I was belly-down on the bedspread, inhaling the rank vapors, the television tuned to a very bad closed circuit porn film. I don't know what's so great about close-ups of dicks going into orifices. I want to see the guys' faces as it's happening. When I wasn't at the pool I was in the room, reading, watching TV, drinking Jack Daniel's, smoking cigarettes and joints, eating burritos with super hot sauce from the Taco Bell across the street, jerking off, lying on the bed imagining the men I'd observed. They'd come into my room, I'd be splayed on the bed. They'd get on top of me, pressing me down. Letting go of everything, I'd watch their faces, feeling my body respond to their attentions, trying to note the exact moment when they reached the threshold of ecstasy and would, for a moment or two, seem to fly away from themselves to return happier, relaxed, wet and gracefully unburdened. Even beasts look beautiful for several moments at a time.

If the motel had more decoration, I could say that it looked tacky. But there was not really much of anything that would merit that distinction. In the lobby sat a nondescript table, a seedy couch and two potted palms. Beyond lay the pool, oval and not very large, a few scattered things to sit and lounge on, all surrounded by dwarf trees, scruffy bushes, lianoid tendrils, pointy swards, creating a fake rain forest within the horseshoe courtyard, surrounded by two tiers of small rooms.

I walked up the concrete steps, clutching the wooden rail, the paint chipped and stained, and moved across the catwalk of upper berths to room number seventeen. There were about twenty-four in all, I think. Just as I placed the key in the lock, a woman, short and slim, speaking heavily-accented English, ran up to me and said that the room hadn't been made up yet, would I wait for about ten minutes? I asked her if I could leave my suitcase in the room and wait by the pool. She didn't understand me so I smiled, walked into the room, put it beneath the television set and said, very slowly, enunciating with great care, that I'd wait downstairs by the pool. She smiled and I went down, into the thick greenery and sat in a chair of metal tubes and cross-hatched bands of multi-colored, faded canvas. There was no one in sight. Nor was there any sunshine. I sighed and lit a cigarette. Just then, a door above opened and a young blond guy in cut-offs and tanktop emerged, hurried across the catwalk, down the stairs and entered the lobby. And a few seconds later a guy from a different room came down and joined me beside the pool. Medium of build, with dark hair, his face didn't look exactly stupid or nerdy but didn't display much awareness, intelligence or cool either. There was something in the way his eyes seemed to wander and a slackness about the mouth that communicated something to me that I can only call uninteresting. I was ready to extend my hand and introduce myself but before I did he asked, in a very nasal voice, if I had any rolling papers that he could borrow so he could roll a joint. I told him that there was a pack in my suitcase, but I'd have to wait until the cleaning lady finished in there before I could go and get it. He seemed very disappointed and started telling me (while I was wondering if I should have called her a chambermaid) about a bar he'd been to the night before. He'd been unable to score and couldn't afford a hustler. I asked where he was from. Las Vegas, he told me. I wondered why he could afford to book a room at this place but couldn't afford a hustler.

The lady came out of the room and hung over the railing. Senor, she called and beckoned me with her hands. I told the guy I'd be right back and ran up the stairs and into the room, opened the suitcase and got out the papers, but when I came back out and looked down at the chairs beside the pool he was gone.

The room had a musty odor, the walls were a yellowish green. Beneath a damp bedspread was a lumpy mattress with an end table at the side near the door. Opposite was a banged-up bureau and a television set on one of those mechanical arms that they have in hospitals that jut out from the wall and can move forward and back, from side to side. The small bathroom had a shower stall, sink, toilet and a window the size of a mass market paperback.

I stripped to my underwear and unpacked. Changed into a swimsuit, locked the room and lay in the cool air beneath the overcast sky.

I work for a firm that distributes office supplies. Acid-Free Microfiche Binders. Custom Engraved Plastic Signs. Pressure Sensitive Labels. Deluxe Heavy-Duty Steel Vertical Files. Lightweight Free Standing Mail Organizers. I'm on the road, actually, in the air, several months a year, a modern Willie Loman, visiting the company's largest clients. My first trip to Los Angeles, I asked a friend where to stay. He suggested the Oasis Motel. Told me it's a gay hotel and I'd feel very comfortable. I imagined it would be something like the gay resorts I've been to, where vacationers go to relax. But this place was more like a public transportation john, most people renting rooms by the hour, checking in and out like the trains arriving to and departing from Grand Central Station.

Before I got off the plane, before I stepped inside the Oasis, I carried in my mind a picture of Los Angeles, images in words from the minds of Chandler and Bukowski. But now, having been there and back, the memory I carry is closer in spirit and style to Genet and Burroughs. William S., not Edgar Rice.

The manbeast moved closer to me. I could finally see his face more clearly. Big eyes set closely together, a squat nose and thick lips. And his body. Large, in keeping with my earlier assessment. But not flabby. My beast, bulky but solid, would have been scorned by my friends, who upon taking in his presence would smirk and chortle, cackle and howl, white crows on the branch of a dead tree passing judgment on all who dared walk by. But this failure, this insult to the gym mentality, this truant from the school of gay male aesthetics turned me on more than any magazine or video model, more than any muscle queen I'd ever seen anywhere. He reminded me of those brutes on television wrestling with their huge chests, enormous arms, big butts, jutting baskets and massive thighs, hunkering in a crouch ready to launch an attack—either sexual or violent, maybe a combination of both. I was a little excited, but also a bit frightened. He sat in a chair beside me. I looked at him and said hi. He extended the joint toward me, his face in a tight, expressionless, but almost mesmerizing stare. I held up my hand in a gesture that said no thank you. He sort of grunted, got up and ambled away, moving like an overstuffed teddy bear, a slow, determined, low-legged gait. I wanted to bury my face between his thighs. But I looked away and rolled over onto my stomach to conceal the swelling in my swimsuit.

I watched the motel guests come and go.

Sometimes a single man would enter a room and over the course of several hours be visited by a succession of young men. I assumed that what went on between them had very little to do with trigonometry or discussion about the Spanish-American War. In other instances, two men would check into a room together, stay for an hour or two, and then leave. In my three days at the Oasis, mine was the only suitcase on the premises, as far as I knew.

I was enjoying myself, watching the all-male parade, and I imagined what their lives were like beyond the walls of the motel. In certain cases I invented entire biographies. Some were, of course, in the entertainment field—movies and television—others belonged to street gangs. A few were businessmen, others were most likely teachers, drug dealers, cops, lawyers, politicians and doctors. They worked, ate meals, had homes, went to the beach, saw movies and watched television. Of this, I was certain. My brute worked as a blue-collar laborer, a plumber, a carpenter or construction worker by day, moonlighting as a masked Mexican superstar of television wrestling, grappling with other brutes in sweaty bouts that were held illegally in makeshift arenas on the poor side of town where the official rule book had been thrown out and each contestant would do whatever it took to defeat and humiliate the other combatant.

I called to confirm an appointment. With Jonathan Collins, Senior Purchaser for the accounting division of a large corporation. Collins asked if I'd meet him for dinner the next evening at a much-talked-about new restaurant and I eagerly consented. Then returned to my favorite chaise by the pool and observed, with fascination, the pageant of horny men.

It became impossible to ignore my own desires. I suppose I might have been able to forget the beast if the activities of the other guests weren't constantly bombarding my consciousness with thoughts of sex. And I didn't know exactly

what it was that finally strengthened my resolve and in-
duced me to take action, but I finally abandoned convention
and tradition, responding to the call of a familiar and usually
ignored voice from somewhere inside of myself.

The courtyard was empty except for me and my observer.
I rose from the chaise, no solar rays binding me to it, and
approached the beast, lurking in the shadows beneath the
catwalk. I imagined his surprise as the distance shrunk
between us. Told myself that he probably thought I was
going to ask him for the correct time or directions to the La
Brea Tar Pits. He looked at me expectantly as I asked if he
wanted to play. To play, he said quizzically and I shook my
head, yes, to play, your room or mine? Yours, he said with a
tentative grin and followed me up the stairs and into the
room.

The shades were closed, the only light coming from a small
lamp on the end table. He stood at the foot of the bed. I asked
him his name but he made no reply. He looked around but
the decor failed to impress him; I could perceive no response.
I'd never been so bold before, had never entered into a
tricking situation without at least a few moments of small
talk, a brief bout of verbal foreplay. I was with the bounty
I'd wanted but wasn't sure what to do next. He helped me
out by moving toward me in that deliberate, arms at the
ready, haunches in a near-crouch stance just like the
wrestlers on television. He touched my hair, tweaked a
nipple, then wrapped me in a tight embrace. He bit my neck,
squeezing me, rubbing up against me. He stepped back,
pulled off his Speedos, then yanked mine down and crouched
at my feet, breathing softly on my dangling cock. With the
first rush of warm air I became erect and felt every nerve
ending in my body become fully attentive, alert for any
sensation that might be felt.

The following night I met Collins for dinner. We'd already
reached an agreement pertaining to our business. This was
to be a symbolic meal, not a haggling session, in which we'd
cement that which had already been decided.

The restaurant, I think it was called Alberta's, is a large

establishment with a fancy four-columned entranceway where you leave your car with a gorgeous blond teenage boy and enter a huge place with a bar up front—all sharp edges of chrome and glass, then an even bigger dining room like a large cave with chunks of terra cotta and remnants and swatches of burlap. As with most people and things in Los Angeles, the exterior is hard but it gets softer closer to the heart. The heart of this place is the kitchen whose chef managed to make some very tasty treats from disparate combinations. Some of the dishes reminded me of an odd recipe from a Flaubert novel: flamingo tongues with pepper and wine.

Collins brought two business associates. One, a slender blond fellow, Art Matewsky, an assistant Vice President, and my beast, Raymond Estella, Accountant-in-Chief. When I saw him sitting at the restaurant table, in a blue suit with a burgundy tie, I didn't know how to respond. Should I acknowledge our prior meeting? When Collins introduced us I could easily have said, we've already met, but I pretended I'd never seen him before. He acted as though he'd never had my cock in his mouth or ass. I relaxed but remained alert for signs that he might somehow reveal our brief but intense encounter. Perhaps another glass of wine might activate his tongue. But he remained very quiet throughout the meal, as taciturn as he'd been at the Oasis, only speaking when it was required, confining his statements to concise rejoinders.

When the meal was over, we all shook hands and said goodbye. The brute gave my hand an extra squeeze, but his eyes, his voice, revealed nothing.

I returned to the Oasis and sat in my room. I could hear the men's voices, footfalls on the catwalk, doors opening and closing just beyond my window. I stretched out on the bed wondering if I'd tell my friends, the disapproving white crows, that I'd been intimate with someone they'd quickly tell me was too ethnic, too old, too fat, too hairy, not good enough for me.

Shortly after my return to New York some minor medical problems resulted in a test which proved my system to be

HIV Positive. The first thing I thought of was the beast. I'd have to contact his firm, ask for Raymond Estella and share with him the most unpleasant message a person can ever be forced to deliver. I recalled how the brute had mauled me into a frenzy, sucked my body's essence until I was empty, how his aromas had made me feel tingly all over, the way his hairy and massive limbs had carried me to a mirage that is real among my memories, reminding me of the last time I was able to experience complete sexual release, something to hold onto until death like a phantom comes.

It's ironic and fitting that the last should be the best, that I finally experienced that which I'd been seeking and avoiding all my life. The California sun never touched me, but something far more satisfying held me close and gave me what I needed—cool water down a parched, gritty throat in a hot, dry desert.

LIFE IS THE ILLUSION

Not long ago before we noticed the coffee tasted strange, Ramona had begun to exhibit signs of unusual behavior. Eating little chocolates, for one. The first time I found the crumpled red foil of a liquid-center chocolate-covered cherry on the floor of her dressing room, I assumed it had been dropped there by one of the youngsters in the cast. Or perhaps a careless visitor. But soon after that I walked in, unintentionally surprised her, and she speedily licked the evidence from the tips of her fingers. She smiled guiltily, looked away, wiped her hands on her jeans, then gazed at me as though nothing out of the ordinary had occurred. But this was the woman who lectured us constantly about over-eating, junk food, too much refined sugar, not enough fiber. Warned us about our teeth, our stomachs, our colons. Ramona had conquered every tidbit of knowledge on the subject of nutrition and health. And had herself become a paradigm of sensible eating and exercising. Always quick to berate one of us for indulging in a forbidden pleasure, it was more than a little disturbing to see her sneaking a bon-bon.

And she'd begun to expound to me a bit less. The play had been running for over eight months and initially we'd not gone through a single costume change together without Ramona lecturing me on theater, art, communication, linguistics, body language. "Life is the illusion, theater is the reality," she would intone. And she'd often say something to the effect that, "Art is what it's all about. Everything else comes second. One couplet from a Shakespearean sonnet is worth more than the entire population of Bombay."

"You don't really believe that," I'd say, zipping up the rear of her ballgown. "You wouldn't say that if you had a child living there, for example."

She sipped mineral water from a bottle, threw back her mane of dark curls and said, "Yes, I do believe it and even if I had a precious child—which I don't—who lived there, I would still believe it. If I didn't how could I go out there six nights and two afternoons a week and murder my mother?"

But this kind of talk had become intermittent, then sporadic, and finally, extinct. Ramona seemed listless, dissatisfied, more on edge, too easily upset. And perhaps, it did have something to do with murdering her mother eight times a week. Not actually committing a crime, of course. But feeling the pain, terror, guilt of such an act down deep in the molecules of her marrow. A truly great actress like Ramona Black would never fake it. And I knew of nothing in her private affairs that could induce the anomie to which she seemed to have succumbed. So I attributed her state of mind to the rigors of the play.

The Madness of the Hour by Tadeusz Wieniewska had been an underground "hit" in Cracow before the authorities closed it down after six performances. A manuscript had been smuggled out and translated into English. After eight months on Broadway—a serious drama in a sea of childish musicals—*The Madness of the Hour* brought as much respectability to the Barrymore Theater on Forty-Seventh Street as it did shame to the Polish officials who'd tried to exterminate it.

And it brought respectability to Ramona Black as well. Not that she'd ever been anything less than a true star, a genuine artist. But the television series she'd been signed to had not made it to the fall schedule, her last Broadway show had run for three performances, and the movie she'd spent nine weeks filming in Iceland had bypassed the theaters and gone straight to the video stores. She'd needed a great part, lots of attention, and the security of a big hit. And she'd found it playing the flamboyant freedom fighter who commits matricide. But the role, in addition to shoring up her confidence and stature, was whittling away at her psyche. And others were beginning to notice. Like Harlan Taylor, the stage manager. And Dulcie Gillis, the young actress who played Ramona's daughter on stage. They'd become my buddies. The only people among the cast, crew, designers and management, aside from Ramona, whom I ever actually talked to—beyond the level of getting the job done. My work takes me to different theaters, introduces me to new faces, and whenever I hook up with a show that lasts for more than a few nights, I usually befriend two or three co-workers. We remain fairly close until the play has run its course. Then we move along and create new families.

Harlan Taylor, as big as a barrel, had only recently started working at the Barrymore. For many years he'd been a stage manager at the Metropolitan Opera. But after that had worn him out he'd moved to Broadway. "Sheeit!" he explained. "Smaller casts, fewer sets, less bull. Makin' less money than before but I'll live longer!" he said, scrunched up his big, brown face, and rolled his shoulders to indicate there was nothing more to be said. Friendly to me, occasionally cantankerous with a snotty actor or producer, Harlan could always be counted on to relate a scandalous backstage tale from the Met, or turn my face red with a truly gross joke. "Anthony," he'd say, and put his arm around my shoulder, "did I tell you the one about the Frenchman, the Englishman and the American who meet in a graveyard?" he'd ask. I could smell the scent of Camels on his breath.

"No," I'd reply.

He'd bring his mouth right to my ear and whisper the lewd punchline. Then I'd blush as red as a ripe tomato and exclaim, "Harlan!" and then I'd laugh so hard I'd be shaking and he'd join me and we'd finally have to stop to catch our breath.

It was Harlan who first befriended Dulcie Gillis and very soon after, the three of us were inseparable between performances on matinee days. She was sixteen during her stay with *The Madness of the Hour* and at first, I thought she was too young to hang out with me. I began by masking my true activities whenever she was around. I'd never make reference to drugs or sex or anything else that might corrupt an innocent youth. But she was bright, wise beyond her years, and it soon became apparent that she was mature enough to handle my pot-smoking and my affairs with men. She asked me to get her some pot once but I declined. That would be going too far. And when she pressed me for details about my sexual experiences I was pretty vague, initially, until she made it clear that there wasn't much she hadn't heard or read about. And from that point on I felt comfortable discussing any topic with her that might arise.

"Did you get laid last night?" she would ask.

"Maybe," I'd say.

"Were you with Todd?"

"Yes."

"Did he fuck you silly?"

Hearing her say this, looking at her Patty Playpal demeanor, would loosen up my sense of propriety.

Then I'd giggle and she'd start to giggle and then she'd go to the coffee maker, fix two regulars, and we'd sip, talking about more serious things. Often, matters dealing with ecological catastrophes.

Ramona could have joined us. Without being too obvious about it, the three of us tried to pull her into our circle. We sensed that she would be sympatico. But she was aloof, ignored our overtures, so we joined hands without her. Though always pleasant and kind, she chose to observe the boundaries that separate the various factions of a theatrical community. Boundaries that, perhaps, Harlan, Dulcie and I should have observed too, but like the anarchists we fancied ourselves, chose to ignore.

Dulcie was the first to notice the coffee tasted odd. We sat in a changing room lined with costumes: a few articles of modern dress, plus frilly, bustly, spangly period things for the fantasy sequences. Harlan was telling me about a certain soprano he'd known. "Sheeit! She swallowed dick morning, noon and night but never strained her throat—never missed a high note!"

Dulcie was the first to bring a steamy mug to her lips. She tasted. Then her face crinkled like a peach pit. "Yuck!" she exclaimed.

I tasted mine. It seemed more bitter than usual.

"I've had much worse," said Harlan.

He finished what was in his mug. Dulcie dumped hers in a toilet. I just left mine on the coffee table.

The next day I fixed myself a mug and it seemed normal. But the day after that it tasted awful. I threw it out. About a minute and a half before her first act entrance, Dulcie grabbed my arm, pulled me into an alcove and whispered, "Don't drink the coffee!"

"Why?"

Her fingers dug deeper into my biceps. "I'm not putting you on," she said as severely as a sixteen-year-old actress can. "It's piss! Ramona's! I saw her pee into the coffee maker!" She stared at me with deadly intensity, defying me to doubt her.

"What do we do?"

"Nothing! Just don't drink anymore. Okay?"

"Okay."

She let go of my arm and the blood began to circulate in my fingers again.

I felt more than a bit uncomfortable dressing Ramona; unzipping the practical skirt, accepting the off-white blouse, helping her step into the eighteenth century French court gown. Was this woman, this brilliant actress, urinating in our coffee? And if so, why? My hands trembled slightly and my fingers fumbled a great deal. "What's wrong with you today, Anthony?" she asked with sweet sincerity.

"Nothing. Just being my usual klutzy self."

"Relax. There's no rush."

"Okay," I said, but my stomach felt swimmy and I had to

really work at it to keep my knees from colliding. I wondered if Dulcie could be mistaken. Or joking. Or—I didn't want to even consider it—just being cruel.

And then I found out the truth for myself one day when I arrived at the Barrymore a few minutes earlier than usual. The table with the coffee maker, sugar, milk, stirrers and mugs is in the green room. I was about to enter when I heard a strange sound. Like the clanging of garbage can lids. My body tensed immediately at the oddness of this noise and I cautiously peered around the door frame instead of just marching in. And there was Ramona, moving the large metal urn from the table to the floor. She glanced up to make sure no one was looking. I backed away in time. Then she surreptitiously took it into her dressing room. I ducked into an alcove. She didn't see me. A few minutes later she returned the coffee maker to its place. Although I hadn't actually seen her hike up her dress and squat, nor had I heard the pinging of her water on metal, I was very certain that Ramona was the culprit.

So, when the company manager accused Dulcie of this crime it was up to me to be the bringer of justice. Another youngster in the cast—Johnny Kincaid—was the first person the manager had accused. But at this point, no one knew that urine was causing the strange taste. It was determined that something was awry and it was assumed that the joker was a youngster. But when confronted and accused of this misdeed, Johnny somehow managed to convince them that he'd had nothing to do with it.

So the prosecutor turned to Dulcie. And, as she told us later, the interrogation went something like this:

"Young lady, have you been tampering with the coffee machine?"

"No."

"Someone is putting something in there that makes it taste funny."

"Urine."

"What?"

"Pee."

26

"Huh?"

"Piss. It's piss."

His face turned six shades of scarlet. "How do you know?"

"I just know."

"Then you must be the one!"

"No, I'm not."

"Then who?"

"Can't say."

She loyally and steadfastly refused to implicate Ramona. Upper management was convinced that Dulcie had done it and they took steps to terminate her contract.

Word spread through the theater's population like a nuclear chain reaction. Within hours of Dulcie's disclosure the oft-repeated message was: Don't drink the coffee. The theater owners instructed Harlan to buy a new coffee maker. And everyone, particularly the actors and actresses, began to whine and moan. How could this outrage have occurred? Isn't there something in the union regulations about this?

Ramona seemed oblivious to the entire affair. Tightening the bodice of her funeral outfit, my heart was slam-dancing against my ribcage as I cautiously asked, "What do you think of the coffee fiasco?" I fully expected her to slap my face, run from the room and have me fired.

But she slid into her grand diva mode and sighed, then casually said, "Of course, you know, I never drink coffee. And, never forget, a great artist must endure many a calamity to survive in this prosaic world."

I decided to see just how far she would take this charade. "Do you have any idea who might have done it?"

She looked me squarely in the eye and said, "Probably some poor soul who's desperate for attention."

I could see that a confession would not be forthcoming. So I went to see the company manager and told him what I knew. He acted like I had to be insane to make such an accusation. "Ramona Black is a star. She'd never do anything like that! Her behavior has always been exemplary!"

"I can prove it," I said and took him to her dressing room. On the mirrored vanity table was an open bag of potato chips. I pointed to the evidence triumphantly. "See! A few months ago she'd have taken her own life before eating something like this. She's going crazy and the coffee maker is just one example of how far out there she's gotten."

He refused to believe me. Must have thought I didn't like Ramona and was trying to get her in trouble or something.

Harlan and Dulcie offered consolation when I told them that I'd tried to clear her name and had failed. Her contract had been terminated and she had less than a week to go before leaving the production. And things had not really gotten back to normal among the cast and crew. Some resumed drinking the coffee with no complaints. But others refused to have any—or if they did—said that it still tasted weird.

Everything changed the day before Dulcie's last show. In the morning, when the early edition of the newspapers became available, the front page headlines shouted the latest celebrity scandal. A Broadway star was named. Ramona Black. The trouble involved a jelly donut at a coffee shop on Forty-Eighth Street. Apparently there was only one donut remaining and Ramona had gotten into a fight with another customer over who would get it. The other person eventually tried to back down but Ramona slugged him. The owner called the police.

The Donut Riot story saturated the theater district before noon. At two o'clock that same day, the new *Playbill* arrived at the theater. The feature article consisted of interviews with actors and actresses who'd forsworn junk food and had gone macrobiotic. The lead quote was attributed to Ramona Black, currently starring in *The Madness of the Hour*. I don't recall the exact wording of the quotation but it was something like, "In a world gone mad how can one pollute one's body with sugar, salt and evil chemicals? The only way to purify the planet is to start with our own bodies."

The man who'd tangled with Ramona did not press charges. But when she arrived at the theater she was told that her behavior was creating a bad image for the show and she'd have to resign or be fired. Her manager had to be summoned to escort her from the Barrymore.

Dulcie's contract was resurrected a few hours later and the company manager apologized to her for his false accusation. The understudy to Ramona, Shelly English, took over the leading role and kept me on as her dresser.

Shelly was not as status-conscious as Ramona and eventually became a part of the Dulcie-Harlan-Anthony social circle. The show continued for only about two months after Ramona's departure, but we were a tight little group and had lots of fun between shows.

On the afternoon of the last matinee, the four of us sat in the green room, joking playfully, to dispel the on-coming gloom that is an appendage to any final curtain. "It's been quite an experience for me," Shelly quipped. "My first starring role on Broadway and my first taste of piss."

Harlan laughed so hard he finally had to stop just to catch his breath.

"I can't believe it," I said, "some of the cast and crew still won't drink the coffee."

"Really?" Dulcie looked at me, amazed. "Like who?"

I began to identify the wary individuals when Harlan harumphed and interrupted me. "Sheeit! This is ridiculous," he roared with a mocking grin. "Half these people got their tongue up somebody's asshole every Saturday night and they're upset about a little piss in their coffee? Sheeit!"

RAZORBACK

Puddles.

I lifted my face from the gutter. Felt the sting where my jaw hit the pavement. Puddles right before my eyes. Slicked over with oil. Alternately yellow and black. Reflecting the stuttering neon sign. Over that doorway. Unfamiliar to me. The sign said "Cocktails." Off again. On again.

I got to my feet. Swaying slightly. I could still feel the pain on the back of my neck where he'd struck me. Karate chop, I guessed. I walked to the sign and peered through the window below it. Inside were rich people and their bodyguards. Talking and drinking. I could have used a drink. But had nothing to trade.

And where was he?

Then I heard the double click. It came from across the street. It was him. And his switchblade. Click. Click. Open and shut. All the time. He came toward me. And pulled aside his tattered lapels. To remind me of the machete suspended from his leather belt. As though I could forget. Involuntarily, my hand reached up to touch my slashed cheek. He held the knife against my other cheek. I felt the point pressing into my skin. I prayed that he wouldn't cut me again. He slapped my face and gestured with his head. That I should follow. I did. Willingly. For even though he was my enemy, he was also my protector. He provided food—well, nothing really tasty or substantial, but at least I hadn't starved to death. And his home—again, not much but four walls and a ceiling cluttered with debris—was where I stayed. And even though he was cruel and would hurt me sometimes, he would allow no one else to mistreat me. That's something, I supposed. But not much, I admitted.

He prodded me in the direction of home. I felt the blunt end of the knife handle between my shoulder blades. I obeyed.

We were crossing one of the broad avenues, dark since someone had shattered the streetlights. I couldn't remember how long it had been since they'd worked. Almost everything was dark at night since the creeps had taken over.

Suddenly, a loner jumped out at us from an alleyway. Brandishing a broomstick. Click. The switchblade was opened. Moonlight glinted off the flat, shiny surface. The loner turned and ran down the alley.

We got home without further incident.

Home was a basement apartment somewhere in what used to be called the midtown area. That was before everyone began to leave. Prior to that, things had gotten steadily worse, but life was tolerable. Then the street gangs took over. They ruled the entire city. Except for a few rich folks who'd decided to stay and could pay for protection. And the loners who'd refused to join a gang or who had quit one. And what was I in this strange and primitive hierarchy? A prisoner and a slave. In service of and protected by a loner. An independent agent whose strength, speed, cunning and luck prevented his becoming another fatality; another un-buried corpse in the city that looked like a ravaged grave-yard.

We lived at the bottom of a metallic stairwell that led from the sidewalk to our door. Several dead-bolt locks were the only thing between us and the creeps. Upon entering, the first noticeable thing was the dank and moldy odor. A couple of stained mattresses on the floor. A naked bulb dangling from the center of the ceiling. Thick curtains over the high windows, taped to the frames so that no light could escape. And on the floor, amid the old clothing, empty cans and spent batteries, hundreds of cassettes and paperbacks.

He locked the door behind us. I sat on my pallet. He removed his raincoat. The kind that British spies always wear in the movies. But his was grimy, spotted, ragged. Just like my clothing. What little I had left.

Beneath the raincoat he wore the T-shirt I'd seen him take off only a couple of times. It was black and he had at one time had letters sewn on it that said "Razorback." I did not know what this meant until I saw his shirtless back one day. A herringbone pattern of scars ran in a broad ribbon from his neck to his waist. He'd either been in a ritual fight, held prisoner and tortured, or had once belonged to a gang. Some of which had pretty weird initiation rites. I never found out because he never said anything. Never even told me his name. So I started calling him Razorback. Not out loud. But in my mind. To keep things organized. I gave him a name just to make things easier for myself.

As usual the first thing he did was heat up a can of soup on the two-burner stove. I always thought that the gas would run out, but like the electricity, it was always available and there was never a bill to pay.

We ate the soup—split pea with ham, as I recall—then he sat on his pallet and put on his headphones. A Walkman, of course. I'm not sure what he listened to, but it was most likely underground rock. By some group with a disgusting name. It didn't make any difference to me. But, as usual, he pointed the machete in my direction, meaning that I should pick up a book and read. Which I did. He never cared what I read as long as the pages kept turning.

So he listened and I read and eventually we both fell asleep. A typical night for us. Not much fun as far as I was concerned. But at least I was still alive.

*

I thought I was a light sleeper, but Razorback was one up on me. If I ever tried to leave my mattress during the night, he was always on his feet with the switchblade open before I could make two strides. So I was unable to overpower him while he slept. It would have been foolish for me to even try because without him I couldn't have lived for very long.

The only thing I knew about was books. And they were as useful to a person in this city as a computer would be to a monkey in the jungle. At some point—how long ago I couldn't say—most people either forgot, or never learned, how to read. There were students like myself, though, who not only knew how but actually enjoyed it. So there came to be a class of "readers" who could be hired by rich people to do their reading for them. And that's what became of me. As soon as I graduated from school I was hired by Mr. and Mrs. Garrison McMartin. They insisted that I move in with them—I had my own room with a fireplace and an air conditioner—and all they expected of me was that I read as much as I could and tell them the plots to all the new novels so they could talk about them at dinner parties and other social affairs. It was heaven for me. But I often wondered about the literary chit-chat at those parties. I mean, if a book is to be discussed only by people who have never read it—well, I guessed a lot of those discussions were pretty funny. But not to those involved. As far as I knew, all of the McMartin's friends had readers too. I think I would have gotten a big kick out of eavesdropping on one of those talks, but I never had the chance.

The McMartins had a huge library of classics—all unread until I came along—and each week they'd pick up a dozen or so new novels. I was kept busy but loved every minute of it. Almost every evening after dinner I'd tell them what I'd read that day. They would listen and ask me to repeat the sexy stuff so they wouldn't make any mistakes when the talk came around to the juicier parts. Then I'd read them the important stories in that day's newspaper.

It wasn't easy adjusting from the McMartins to Razorback. I used to live in the finest of surroundings with excellent food and the literature of the world at my fingertips. And then quite suddenly I found myself in a dingy basement eating canned soup and forced to re-read the same books over and over.

I haven't quite figured out what Razorback hoped to get from me. Unlike the McMartins, he never asked me about the books I read. He was content as long as my face was pointed at small print and pages turned. Was I some kind of status symbol? Did he believe that having his own private reader would somehow make him better than the other loners? I didn't know. He never said and I never asked.

When he captured me and dragged me to his apartment I automatically assumed that he had something sexual in mind. I was correct. He fucked my ass with wild abandon. We were standing up with our pants bunched around our ankles. I've always enjoyed rough action. I jerked my cock as he pumped me. It was fine. Every now and then, without warning or preamble, he'd pull our pants down and do me. It was a change from our routine. I didn't worry too much about sexually transmitted diseases. He probably didn't either. There were greater dangers around most corners and behind many doors.

In the mornings I felt disoriented. Must have been the nightmares. I had grown used to pleasant dreams and idyllic mornings with hot coffee, buttery croissants and sunshine pouring through my window. But at Razorback's the mornings were dark and smelly. Breakfast simply didn't exist.

I'd open my eyes and Razorback would be sitting cross-legged on his mattress, polishing his machete. Actually, it was just a large butcher knife. But in his artful hands it became a machete, a sabre, a scythe. He'd glance over at me while rubbing the blade with a chamois, and gesture—with his chin—at the books on the floor. I'd pick one up and start to read. But it was so difficult to concentrate so early. I'd still be recalling bits and pieces of scary dreams, trying to figure what they meant and what caused them. Some of the images would keep returning.

I'd be in a car that was under water and all the doors and windows were locked. I couldn't open them and water was seeping in, rising higher and higher. It always ended with me kneeling on the front seat, my head thrown back, gasping for the shrinking bubble of air just beneath the roof. I'd try to breathe one more time and my lungs would fill up with cold water. Then I'd wake up.

Or I'd be standing with my back to a wall and a gang of creeps would be closing in. First they'd cut off one of my arms. Then one of my eyes would be plucked out. Toes were chopped off one at a time. Then the gang leader would hold his sword at my groin. He'd lift his arms in an upward arc. I'd scream. And wake up.

All this while I was trying to read about some wealthy Englishman attempting to marry off his daughters to obnoxious landowners. It all seemed so trivial compared to drowning and disembowelment.

*

I recall awakening. And the stench of decaying human flesh. A horrible odor. Almost certain to induce vomiting. That is, if there's anything in your stomach. I was lying in the gutter, my face pressed against a rotting thigh. Gender? Unimportant. How long since the demise? Difficult to determine. And besides I didn't care.

But I finally figured out Razorback's logic. It was the second time that he'd karate-chopped me into oblivion, leaving me sprawled in the street. It was a form of protection. Razorback, with his swift legs and street-smarts, could easily avoid the creeps and other loners. I, slow and ignorant by comparison, would have been killed instantly. Had the enemy not thought I was already dead. Razorback's method for keeping me alive while we were out scavenging was simple: when in the vicinity of enemies, he would knock me out and leave me sprawled where I dropped. Anyone passing by would take me for dead and leave me alone. Good thing he never hit me hard enough to kill me; just enough to immobilize me and fool the others. I could have pretended I was dead, but I guess that never entered his mind.

So I eventually got used to those strange awakenings. Sometimes in puddles of rain and excrement. Sometimes among slashed corpses. The waking was always brutal. But I was still alive.

Every day we'd venture out of the apartment to search for whatever we could find that might be useful—food, bottled water, batteries. The most costly and rare commodity was condoms but they were increasingly difficult to find. All of the drug stores had been looted a long time ago. An unused condom commanded a higher price than fresh vegetables or coffee.

After Razorback cleaned his weapons and I read for a while, we'd wander the streets. Enter burnt-out department stores and unlocked apartments. We'd find a few cans of food here, perhaps some usable clothing there. Razorback would tear apart any battery-operated toy or appliance he could find. He was hoarding size AA batteries for his Walkman. I assumed that the ultimate horror for him would be to run out of battery power and be left without loud music.

We'd ransack the streets and buildings, gingerly stepping over corpses with spilled entrails. Racing from shadow to shadow, ears cocked, listening for the sounds of hostile creeps approaching.

Razorback was an athlete of evasion. He could hear a gang of creeps from several blocks away and without even seeing them, decide if he should run, take cover or stand and fight. If it was another loner, he'd usually knock me out, ambush the guy and take whatever spoils he considered usable. Then he'd come and pull me from whatever carnage or garbage I'd been left in for safe-keeping.

But one time—I recall it so vividly—Razorback made an error in judgment. It was the beginning of his end. And perhaps mine as well.

We were steeling down a narrow street moving west. Running from doorway to doorway, returning home after a long day's hunt. All was quiet. The sky was gray and the air thick with mugginess.

When we reached the intersection, Razorback peered around the corner. He motioned with his machete that I should follow. We sprinted across the street and ducked into what was left of a burnt-out greengrocery. Razorback foraged in the darkness—I could hear him rifling through cartons, all probably empty—while I kept my eyes on the door. Above the rustling of cardboard we suddenly heard the sound of several pairs of feet on pavement. Razorback stood and cocked his head. Listening. Before we knew it, three creeps burst through the door. Most likely what was left of a ten-to-fifteen-member gang. I automatically got down to the floor and lay as though I were dead. I would have had as much success fighting those guys as a pampered poodle versus a pit-bull terrier. Through half-closed eyes I could see what was happening.

One of the creeps was tall and thin with a shaved head. The second had an average build and long, stringy hair. The third was fat, limped and was missing half of his right arm.

We were invisible in the dark. I lay on the floor in a patch of rotten fruits and vegetables—the odor was almost intoxicating—and Razorback crouched behind an overthrown table. While the creeps waited for their eyes to adjust to the dark, Razorback pounced. With one swift motion he took the head off the fat one-armed guy. Blood hissed out of his neckless torso and the head—with tongue lolling through clenched teeth—rolled until it stopped inches away from my face. I gagged. The tall one turned to see what was happening and Razorback plunged his knife right through the guy's stomach and twisted it clockwise. The creep dropped his knife, tried to hold his guts in with both hands, then tottered and fell. The longhair—quicker than the other two—realized what was going on and backed away, cutting the air with his knife. Razorback approached him, his knees bent, ready to spring. Their knives clashed and the scratching sound of metal on metal made my teeth hurt. While keeping the creep's knife busy, thrusting at him, Razorback reached into his pocket for his switchblade. He pulled it out, clicked it open and raked it across the other guy's face. He howled and licked the blood from his lips as Razorback moved in and drove his knife into the guy's chest. As he pulled it out and backed away, the creep—with his last burst of strength—

thrust his knife deep into Razorback's leg. He fell and crawled away. The creep stopped breathing as Razorback slowly pulled the knife from his calf. Blood dribbled over the blade. He tore off his shirt and tied it around the gushing wound.

I got up and went to him.

He looked up at me. The pain in his eyes was unbearable. I helped him to his feet and draped his arm around my neck. We moved to the door. He gasped as he dragged his punctured leg.

I stuck my head out the door and made certain there were no others. We moved quietly from doorway to shadow. I prayed that we'd get back home without another attack.

We did. Finally. I locked the door behind us and helped Razorback to his mattress. He was shivering and sweating, his face contorted from the pain.

I tore off the bloody shirt and tied a fresh one around his calf. Then I covered him with a blanket and tucked it around him.

I went to sleep but kept waking up. Razorback was having nightmares and would scream something then clutch at his leg. I wished that I could give him something for the pain, but there was nothing. We both slept—on and off—for I don't know how long.

*

I'm not exactly sure how or why everything began to fall apart. Once I'd been installed at the McMartin's I was pretty much cut off from the general flow of life and information. Almost all that I knew was what I heard on the radio, saw on television or read in the newspaper. The rest I picked up from the McMartin's dinner conversations.

If I remember correctly, the decay sequence went something like this. It started with a bunch of newspaper offices and radio and television stations getting sabotaged. The rumors floating around suggested that employees of the various media companies were angry about the news reportage. They claimed it was inaccurate when not brazenly biased. The firebombs flew. The output of the established news sources became sporadic and a bunch of underground newspapers and pirate radio stations suddenly came into prominence. But most of that news was really propaganda.

Shortly after the news became even more of a joke than it had already been, groups of people began to move out. It was said that most went to the country where people were less threatening and you could grow your own food. First the politicians left, then the doctors. The police and firemen soon followed. The subways turned into danger zones where entry was an invitation to death. I supposed it was underground that a lot of gangs formed and trained themselves to become death squads.

The bus drivers eventually disappeared and the taxi drivers were next. It became impossible to get gasoline and a lot of surface vehicles were simply left where they stopped when their gauges pointed to empty.

Life with the McMartins slowly went from luxurious to austere. And the dinner conversations became guarded and scary. Eventually they stopped asking me what I'd been reading. It was plain that they were more concerned with where the next roast or pecan pie would come from. Mr. McMartin owned a chain of restaurants and was able to stockpile alcohol and food. But after he'd traded all of that away and Mrs. McMartin had traded her jewelry and furs for tranquilizers and analgesics, I knew something would have to happen.

One night while we were eating—an assortment of canned vegetables and stale breads—Mr. McMartin announced that we were to leave for the country in a few days.

The country! I was so excited. I packed up my clothes and started bundling my books. I dreamed about tall trees, flower gardens and mountain streams.

On the morning of our departure we gathered in the lobby of the McMartin's building with all our belongings in suitcases and cartons. A panel van with armed guards pulled up to the curb and we started moving our stuff down the steps and onto the sidewalk.

It was a wickedly uncomfortable day and after carrying several loads all of us sat down on the steps to catch our breath and cool off. I opened one of my boxes and took out a book. Mr. McMartin was wiping his forehead with a hanky, Mrs. McMartin was fanning her face with a pamphlet of some sort. I began to read.

Suddenly, I heard gun shots. I looked up in time to see one of the armed guards hit the sidewalk as a gang of creeps descended upon us. They killed the other guard and were taking Mr. and Mrs. McMartin as hostages when one of the gang members—Razorback—approached me. He clicked open his switchblade and carved a small crescent in my cheek. He picked up the carton of books and handed it to me, then held the blade at my throat while he led me around the corner. I guessed the other gang members were having so much fun torturing the McMartins and shooting up the van, they didn't notice that we'd disappeared.

The blood was dripping down my cheek but both hands were full and I couldn't wipe it away. Razorback took me to his basement apartment. We entered and he locked the door behind us. He gestured with his knife and I learned to respond. Quickly. I sat on the mattress that he indicated. He handed me a book opened to the first page. While I read, trembling, wondering what was to become of me, he did push-ups and sit-ups on the floor. Then he cleaned his weapons while listening to his Walkman. Later on he heated up some soup and we went to sleep soon after.

That was the first night since I was a child that I was tormented by nightmares. I haven't had a peaceful night since.

*

Someone or something tickled me. My foot quivered as something soft and wet moved against it. I opened my eyes. It was a rat. Dark gray and slimy. I yelled and kicked it. It scampered into a dark corner.

I lay there for a while. Trying to sort everything out. I realized that I hadn't heard any gun shots in a long time.

No more ammunition, most likely.

I got up and looked at Razorback. He was in a deep sleep. I moved toward him and he didn't spring up at me like I expected. I felt his forehead. He was burning with fever.

I opened a can of soup and heated it. Then I woke him up and made him eat it. Afterwards he went to sleep again. I spent the day reading and worrying.

If Razorback died I would be on my own. The way things stood, I wouldn't last very long. I couldn't really defend myself. I was not very fast. And though I knew a great deal about literature, I knew nothing about survival in the streets.

Time slowed down. I had too much time to think. Would I dare to leave the apartment and look for bottled water? Perhaps I could find some medication so Razorback would get better. I thought about this but was afraid to go out alone.

One night I woke up after a particularly brutal nightmare—I was being attacked by an army of rats with sharp teeth and evil eyes. Sweating all over I got up and paced back and forth. I decided that I would try to become proficient with Razorback's knives. I practiced throwing them until they would lodge tightly into whatever targets I selected. I ruined a lot of paperbacks but I'd already read them and there were plenty more.

During the afternoons I did push-ups and sit-ups. At first it was a real struggle to do even one. But after a few days I could do several with no effort. Day by day I increased the numbers. My body began to harden and I grew more confident.

One morning after I'd served Razorback his soup, he sat up and looked around. His leg was swollen and his face was gaunt. A horrible odor emanated from his body and mattress. He got to his feet and limped to the pantry. We had less than fifteen cans of soup by then. He gathered his weapons and moved to the door. I tried to stop him but he pushed me away. I tried to follow but he threatened me with his machete.

He left and I haven't seen him since. I waited for a few days, but eventually gave up hope. He was in no condition to protect himself and was probably lying in a puddle of his own blood somewhere.

Although I prayed for his return, I realized I was being foolish. He was gone. I was on my own. My body was stronger than it had ever been, but I didn't have any weapons. If I left the apartment I was most certainly doomed. If I stayed, I'd starve. But maybe, I thought, just maybe I'd get lucky. Perhaps I could travel from shadow to shadow and get out of the city. It was possible, but not very probable.

Then I began to think about the possibility that maybe someday I might be rescued. Perhaps there were people somewhere who were planning to return and re-claim the city. I mean, the city was still usable. Most of the buildings stood where they'd always been. Pipes and wiring were largely intact. The main problem, as far as I could see, would be to clean up the carnage in the streets. All the city really needed was some heavily armed people to come and make it work again.

On some days I fantasized about going to the country. On others I'd daydream about an army coming to restore the city to its former stature. And another possibility occurred to me: that if I waited long enough all the creeps would kill each other off, or at least reduce their numbers enough so that I might get out of the city unharmed.

Maybe tomorrow I'll try to escape. Or maybe a week from now. But I could get killed days or moments before someone might come to save me. My dilemma. To leave or to stay. It's hard to decide. There's not much soup left, but I've still got plenty of books to re-read.

BROTHERHOOD

Gregory gets on a plane at LaGuardia airport in New York. A few hours later he lands in South Florida. Takes a taxi to his brother's home in Boca Raton. He is greeted by Candi, his sister-in-law.

After she kisses Gregory on the cheek he enters the house. "Theodore will be home soon from golf," she says.

"How have you been?" asks Gregory.

"Just great. And you?"

"Great. Everything's great."

"How's your…" Candi does not know whether to say lover, roommate, friend, or companion.

"Darrell."

"Right. Darrell. How is he?"

"Fine. Where are Richie and Sherry?"

"Summer camp."

"Summer camp? Where?"

"Vermont."

Gregory thinks it's strange that people would send their kids to someplace other than Florida to have a good time. He thinks Florida itself is one huge summer camp.

They sit in the enclosed patio. Candi and Theodore call it a Florida room.

"Would you like a drink?" Candi asks.

"What are you having?"

"Nothing."

"I don't want anything either."

"How about some water?"

"Okay."

Candi rises to get two glasses of ice water. Gregory wanders about the house. It is a one-story structure with a large living room which fans out into the kitchen, dining room, bedrooms and bathrooms. Every square inch of the floor is plushly carpeted. The decor is a splash of tropical pinks, greens, yellows. Deft use of black and white makes it appear still more colorful.

Theodore arrives and greets his brother. Then his wife.

Dinner is served at six o'clock. Candi removes dishes from the microwave and brings them to the table.

"About tomorrow," says Theodore, one year and three months older. Gregory looks up expectantly. He's been avoiding this for over ten years, since Theodore and Candi left New York and settled in Florida to raise Sherry and Richie. "We rise when the rooster crows."

"No problem," says Gregory. He will visit the club his brother and sister-in-law have been boasting about. He will tell them how lovely it is. And with the obligation met, he'll never have to return. "What's new?"

Theodore grins. "New television, new car, new microwave, next month we're painting the Florida room."

"That's nice," says Gregory.

Everyone smiles.

In the morning they have breakfast in the sparkling white kitchen. Gregory, Theodore and Candi sit at the round table. Orange juice, poached eggs, toast and decaf.

Gregory looks helplessly at Candi. "Um, do you have any real coffee? You know, with caffeine?"

As Candi is about to apologize, Theodore says, "Don't you know what caffeine does to your system? It's poison! Why I read somewhere that every cup of caffeinated coffee you drink takes thirteen minutes off the rest of your life."

Gregory lights a cigarette. "If I want to take thirteen

minutes off the rest of my life that's my privilege."

"I'm so sorry," says Candi.

"It's all right."

"I didn't know," she adds.

"Really, it's okay. I'll live."

"Not if you keep poisoning your bloodstream, you won't."

"Let's not fight," says Gregory.

They eat silently.

Afterwards Candi cleans up. Theodore has to go to the store to pick up a few things for dinner. Gregory goes for a walk.

The home of Theodore and Candi is located in a housing development called Palmetto Springs. But this is quite unlike any real estate configuration that Gregory has observed anywhere. In the center of Palmetto Springs is a Golf and Tennis Club which boasts four eighteen-hole courses and thirty-six courts. The homes are situated on plots of land bordering the green fairways. Built especially for golf and tennis enthusiasts, the homes offer them the advantage of being able to arrive at the first tee or court number one in the time it would ordinarily take you to reach the first of many red lights.

Part of the arrangement is that the homeowners never have to worry about their grounds. Teams of landscapers and gardeners continually work on everyone's lawns and backyards so that the entire development has a uniform look. Theodore likes the idea of never having to mow the lawn. Candi likes the consistency and never having to worry that the neighbor's yard will become overgrown and unkempt.

Gregory leaves the house and walks a few blocks, observes some lovely rock gardens, cobbled paths, man-made waterfalls surrounded by garlands of brightly colored flowers. The streets are named after birds. Shirtless, tanned, muscular young men run around with rakes, hoes, hoses and mowers. There are grapefruit, lime, and avocado trees, palms and knees of cypress. Gregory walks around to the backyard of his brother's house. There is a clump of trees he cannot

47

identify. He approaches and hears soft human noises. Getting closer he can see movements within the shadows. Stealthily looking and listening, he inches closer and sees two young men on the ground, slurping each other's cocks. He watches for a few seconds, grins and walks back around to the front entrance of the house.

Candi asks, "Did you have a nice walk?"

"Very interesting."

Theodore returns home with bags of groceries. Then he and Gregory go to the clubhouse in the golf cart. "So, you're still living with Donald?" says Theodore.

"Darrell."

"Sorry, Darrell." Theodore sighs. "I know you have these urges, you just have to try to control them."

"They're not simply urges. They're the core of my existence."

"The core of your existence is making Mom and Pop spin in their graves."

Gregory becomes indignant. "How the hell do you know? Did they send you a postcard or something?"

Theodore does not respond. He knows that unless he is silent the discussion will devolve into a nasty argument.

The route to the clubhouse is like a fairytale illustration. Neat pastel homes nestled in green bowers with palm fronds swaying lazily and bright flower petals spicing the verdure.

The main building of the clubhouse—attached to the Pro Shop, cart shed, and caddy bench— is a large brick edifice with white columns and gingerbread trimming. They park the golf cart and enter. Theodore says, "This is the best that America has to offer. Everyone is honest, fair and family-oriented."

"By family-oriented you mean heterosexual?" Gregory asks as a man in a pink jumpsuit with a purple scarf sashays by.

"Yes," Theodore affirms.

"Interesting," says Gregory. "When I was in New Orleans I saw a drag show in which one of the queens was dressed just like that."

Theodore glances at the man in pink and purple. "The latest in modern golfing fashion."

"Southern gutter drag circa 1977."

Theodore shoots a disapproving look.

Gregory smirks.

They walk through the lobby, down the hall lined with trophies in glass cases and enter the dining room. The host smiles and leads them to a table by the window, looking out over gracefully terraced lawns.

"This is very nice," says Gregory.

Theodore smiles triumphantly.

A waiter appears and hands out menus. Gregory stares at the waiter's eyes. The look is returned. Theodore stares at the menu.

"Our specials today include quiche a la Boca, mock turtle soup and steak au poivre."

Gregory can't resist the urge to be wicked. He looks at Theodore. "Quiche? At an all-American joint like this? I thought real men—"

"I'll have the quiche a la Boca," Theodore interrupts.

"A real man like you?" mocks Gregory.

"It's the latest thing," says Theodore.

"Steak," says Gregory. "Medium."

"Anything to drink, gentlemen?"

"Coffee," says Gregory.

"Perrier," says Theodore.

Gregory raises his left eyebrow. The waiter retrieves the menus and leaves.

Gregory smirks. "Pink jumpsuits, quiche a la Boca, Perrier...what's happening to the land of the brave and the home of the free?"

"Just shut up! Okay? Shut up!"

The meal is consumed in silence. Over coffee, Gregory tells Theodore that the food is wonderful and thanks him.

Theodore shows Gregory the newly renovated mens' locker room. Rows of metal lockers, rows of benches, rows of shower nozzles, rows of sinks and mirrors, stacks of towels, shelves of deodorant, powder, shaving cream, aftershave, combs, razors, cologne, men in towels, men naked, men turning under spitting spigots, men slapping men's behinds, steam, tile, male camaraderie. Theodore raises his arms and says, "This is really something, huh?"

"Yes, Theo, it most certainly is."

Gregory drives the golf cart while Theodore plays nine holes. The terrain offers a smooth ride, the awning atop the cart provides relief from the sun. Theodore is happy chasing tiny white balls and Gregory is content to follow and relax. Theodore slices into the woods to the left of the fairway. While helping to search for the lost ball, Gregory observes a young caddy and an older player, jerking each other's cocks behind a tall hedge. He smiles and turns away.

"Got it!" shouts Theodore, holding the ball aloft. Gregory emerges into the sunlight. They continue to follow the course and eventually return to the clubhouse.

Theodore takes a shower.

Gregory wants to visit the sauna first.

As Theodore is soaping himself, Gregory is settling onto the wooden bench in the hot, steamy, tiled room. There are several men already there, in pairs. Gregory closes his eyes for a moment, then inhales deeply. He feels a hand tentatively pawing at his crotch. He opens his eyes and finds a man with a mustache pushing aside the towel, grabbing for his cock. Gregory looks around, and through the mist can see hands on cocks stroking furiously. He indulges in a quick one then leaves the sauna. He showers and towels himself dry. Then meets Theodore in the lobby of the clubhouse.

They drive the cart back home. "Quite a sauna," says Gregory.

Theodore is pleased that Gregory has said something complimentary.

"Do you use it much?" Gregory asks.

"I don't like the idea of a bunch of men sitting around with nothing on," says Theodore.

"Horrible thought," says Gregory.

They pass the Olympic-sized pool adjacent to the clubhouse. Theodore brags about the swimming competitions held there every Fourth of July. Gregory's attention drifts away from his brother's words and he notices a very-well-muscled, very tanned, very sexy lifeguard by the pool. He looks at the man's blond hair, his sculpted features, his powerful body.

They arrive home by six. Candi serves dinner about forty-five minutes later.

Afterwards, Theodore asks Gregory if he'd like to watch *Woodstock*. They have a videocassette. Gregory politely declines and asks if he can borrow the car.

"Where would you like to go?" asks Candi.

"To a bar."

"Oh," she says, delighted, "which one?"

"Rawhide."

"I haven't heard of it," she says, eager to hear all about it.

Theodore punctures her balloon. "It's a gay bar, honey."

"Oh," she says, embarrassed, "that's okay. I don't mind."

Theodore sighs. "You don't understand, he wants to go alone."

"Oh! I see. That's okay. Really. I don't mind."

"See you later."

Gregory enters the darkness of Rawhide, about a ten minute drive from Palmetto Springs.

The first thing he notices is the lifeguard he'd seen earlier at the clubhouse pool. He's dancing with another sexy, blond, tanned guy beneath the whirling disco globe. Gregory looks around. This bar is unlike the ones he's been to in New York. It combines the high-tech decorative touch of a disco with the gritty raunch atmosphere of a leather bar.

Gregory drinks orange juice instead of scotch because he will have to drive back to the house. He almost goes home with a young local but decides it's too late, he's too tired, and so he leaves alone.

On Sunday morning Candi doesn't start breakfast until almost ten o'clock. When Gregory wakes up she's just begun. He can smell bacon frying. Wriggling into a shirt and shorts he goes to the kitchen.

"Good morning," says Candi.

"Good morning."

"Did you have a good time last night?"

Gregory lifts his hair from his forehead, stirs some milk into his coffee. He drinks it. "Hey! There's caffeine in here!"

Candi smiles.

"Thank you. I had a good time. How was the movie last night?"

"Still my favorite," she says. "In spite of all the mud. Everytime I see it I'm transported back in time. Those were wonderful years."

"They were."

A few minutes later Theodore appears, tying the belt of his Japanese print robe.

"Good morning," he says to no one in particular. Then to Gregory, "What time are you scheduled to leave?"

"If it's all right with you I think I'll stay for a few more days."

Theodore is shocked. "I thought you couldn't wait to check into that sex hotel in Fort Lauderdale. You have a reservation for today, right?"

"Right. But I thought I'd change it and stay for a while. Just a few days. If it's okay."

"Of course it's okay," beams Candi. "We'd love to have you."

"Thank you," says Gregory.

"So," says Theodore, his chest puffed up with victory. "It isn't so bad here, is it?"

"No," says Gregory, recalling the gardeners fucking in the backyard.

"It's clean and wholesome," adds Theodore.

"I can't argue with that," says Gregory, thinking suddenly of the men in the sauna.

"So what are your plans for today?" Candi asks.

"Think I'll go swimming," says Gregory, picturing the hunky lifeguard.

Theodore sighs. "Water, sunshine, golf, tennis…Florida's a far cry from New York."

"But not quite as far as you might think," says Gregory.

THE SOLAR HUNKS FROM URANUS

Captain Pulsar switched his hand-laser from coma to death, planted his legs firmly, aimed at the approaching solar hunk and fired. A needle of white light burned a perfect hole through his scrofulous chest and the solar hunk, emitting a piercing cry, fell forward and expired. As the vapor of life seeped from his prostrate form, the orange color of his lumpy skin began to darken and dull. But the radioactive aura, emanating from every muscled curve of the hunk's dead body, continued to glow, as it would until the half-lives of the radioactive particles were no longer detectable without sensory extenders.

"Damn Quarkbusters!" said Captain Pulsar.

His real name was Li Che Po; that was before he became an intergalactic superstar. Now he's known everywhere as Captain Pulsar.

When he first said the word—quarkbusters—I had no idea what it meant. Sure, I knew what a quark was and I imagined what the act of busting one might look like. I even tried to picture a being who would be occupied with such an enterprise. But, I confess, I wasn't really certain what this caper was about until it was almost over.

The Captain and I, trying hard to maneuver our way through the sprawled bodies of dead solar hunks without touching them, eventually got out of the smooth, shiny corridors of the alien vessel. We believed that if we'd touched—even for one nanosecond—the skin of one of those creatures, we'd be destined for early cremation. If an ordinary human had physical contact with a solar hunk, the radiation would slowly permeate—and eventually kill him, her or it. As attractive as the solar hunks could be, what with their superb musculature and all, if they managed to entice someone into a sexual liaison, the result would be a slow, painful death after a thrilling libidinal experience. Even though the skin of a solar hunk is not particularly enticing (at least to me), the muscles usually cause an ordinary mortal's resolve to dissipate. Then the hormones begin to flow. And like a meteor plummeting to a gravity enclave, the human locks loins with the solar hunk, experiences several moments of divine pleasure, then begins to expire like a bombarded neutrino.

The Captain and I managed to escape from this particular encounter uncontaminated. Not a single one of those over-cooked mutants from Uranus managed to touch us even momentarily.

We entered the air-lock and strapped ourselves into our two-seater shuttle. The Captain maneuvered us away from the alien ship just quickly enough so that when it exploded we were far away; there was no serious damage to our conveyance from the fiery, missile-like debris.

When we docked and disembarked, we made our way to the conference room. I seated myself before the main computer terminal and booted the system as the Captain summoned the Executive Council.

Adam, the first to arrive, greeted us with warmth. "A bit too much," the Captain told me later. "We'll have to have his connections and circuits examined when we get back to Corporation headquarters."

Entering the quiet and cool, plushly decorated conference room with its large table and swivel chairs, Adam first addressed the Captain with a salute, then dropped his pose of formality and hugged him passionately. The Captain grimaced, and finally pushing Adam away said, "Adam, I'm happy to see you too, but I've only been gone for a couple of hours and I only have one set of ribs."

Adam faked a shudder and stood at attention. "Sir? Am I to understand that you do not wish to be hugged?"

The Captain grinned. "No. It's not that." He hesitated for a moment. The Captain had many Asian ancestors and it was part of his nature, a racial trait some say, to be as humble in one's speech as one is aggressive in battle. "You must remember that those arms of yours can crush a real human like a gorilla could a sparrow."

"Certainly, sir, and please accept my apologies."

Adam turned to approach me. Most of the earlier models from Adam's creators walked a bit stiff-legged. But his rolling gait was almost human. With his soft, blond hair, delicate features and intense eyes, he was quite attractive. For a cyborg. While I was conscious of his beauty I was not compelled to desire him because my few sexcapades with cyborgs had all been frustrating. Who wants to go on a date with a creature who can orgasm every thirty seconds? Kind of makes an ordinary guy like myself feel a bit inadequate.

"Bart," said Adam as he hugged me, mindful of the Captain's words, ever so lightly, "was it a successful mission?"

"Yes. We're alive. It was successful."

"Very good."

Adam moved to the far end of the conference table and sat. Moments later Lieutenant Lucille Hopkins and Sergeant Garcia arrived, completing the Executive Council. They sat and Garcia poured himself a glass of water. Lieutenant Hopkins, Lucille, signed to the Captain that she was ready. The Captain looked at Garcia and he nodded.

As the Captain briefed them on our mission aboard the alien ship, I sat and watched Lucille. She has been deaf since birth and is an excellent lip-reader, in addition to having the most graceful signing technique I've ever seen. When someone is speaking to her she watches every movement of the lips and mouth with her big, brown eyes and if you look at her face you see the sweetest most attentive expression you can imagine. I can watch her endlessly. Her face is like an angel's. Her hands are like a sculptor's. With her dark, brown hair and lithe figure, she is quite an attractive person. Sometimes I think that if she were a man or if I were a woman...but I'm happy being me and she's content with herself so...even though we easily could, I don't think either of us wants to make the change.

Anyway, the Captain told the Council how we managed to sneak aboard the solar hunks' vessel and just managed to escape, once they'd detected our presence.

"Regrettably," the Captain wound up his speech, "we were unable to locate the coordinates of their mothership but at least we got rid of about a dozen of them...and we escaped without any injuries to the team or damage to the shuttle whatsoever. Right, Bart?"

"Yes," I confirmed. "And now that we've seen the interior of one of their ships, we'll be better prepared the next time."

Garcia, Security Queen, slammed his big fist on the table. "If I'd been with you, Captain, I'd've pulverized every one of 'em, and their little ship too!"

When he hit the table it felt like the whole room shook. Garcia is a big man, over three hundred pounds of fighting muscle. And when he gets angry it's best to be on his side of the disagreement, or if that's not possible, very far away.

"We needed you here," said the Captain.

"Aye, sir, but next time..."

"What's our next move?" asked Adam.

"Uranus."

Adam blushed, his white android complexion turning to a vague pink. "Captain!"

"The planet Uranus."

"Oh," said Adam, abashed.

Garcia laughed. Lucille shook her head and grinned. I wasn't certain whether Adam had truly misunderstood or if he was just trying to be cute. With cyborgs it's often hard to tell. Captain Pulsar chuckled and ordered us to resume our duties. He called the bridge and asked the space mapper to find the best route to Uranus. After we filed out of the conference room, Garcia took me aside and asked if I was free to fuck for a while. I told him I had to log my report but could meet him about an hour later. He grunted and asked if he should come to my cabin or if I should go to his. I suggested that we meet in the aft air-lock because I knew that he was as fond of anti-grav sex as I.

"Good thinkin'," he said.

There is something quite special about fucking in zero Gs. Those little discomforts that result from sex in normal circumstances simply never materialize. Although I serve the Captain and the good ship Indigo in many capacities—historian, theorist, tale-teller, jester, philosopher and sommelier—I still have time for the occasional sexfest, so I'm not exactly what one might call virginal or inexperienced. Nor am I a profligate—but I'll leave all that to future historians. In any case, I know how it feels when your sex partner accidentally pinches a nerve or crushes a limb beneath his weight—intentional pain is an entirely different matter. When fucking in free-fall this ceases to be a problem. The only thing you have to watch out for is bumping into the walls, floor or ceiling. And it's hard to tell which is which once gravity is no longer a factor. When one is completely involved in a sexual encounter one tends to forget that one might be drifting head-first toward a wall of heavy metal. Sergeant Garcia and I wore helmets, in addition to tiny breathing capsules, and tried to stay at the center of the air-lock. We drifted of course, but never made contact with any undesired hard objects. Garcia's body is hard in all the right places, but his almost gymnastic expertise allows him to utilize his full strength without causing any unwanted bodily damage. After I did the best I could to satisfy myself with his various surfaces and orifices, he did the same with me. I like a guy who's strong and a little rough, so I was completely sated by the time he was finished with me. I felt like I'd been fucked into the middle of the next century, so I was feeling good all over when we felt the first tremors.

"What's that?" Garcia asked.

"Beats me," I replied.

He grinned. "All you ever think about is sex."

Before I could respond to his pun, an admittedly slight exaggeration, the Captain's voice surged from the ship's sound system. "We are under attack by another Uranian vessel. All hands to battle stations. Condition Crimson."

Garcia, trained to respond immediately to such commands, had grabbed his uniform and was gone before I could figure out where I should go. During attacks I was sometimes needed on the bridge, sometimes at my terminal and occasionally I was told to just disappear, be quiet and await further instructions.

After slipping into my uniform I ran to the bridge to see if I was wanted there. As I emerged from the sphincter the Captain shouted, "To the navigator's station! Channel computer dispatches!"

"Aye, aye, sir," I barked and left, running to carry out my orders.

The ship was vibrating from the blows of the enemy laser torpedoes as I reached navigation. Chief of Navigators, Mina Mtume, sat at her console, staring with menacing intensity. She is a short, olive-skinned woman, occasional lover of Lucille, and the best navigator to ever graduate from the Academy. It was her job to try to dodge the salvos from the aliens. With the aid of a computer, she must strategically maneuver our ship through short evasive paths—as during an attack—or plot vast routes that will take the Indigo to the far reaches of the universe.

I sat at the assist console across from her and tried to keep one eye on her, in case she had to signal me, and one eye on the assist screen in case any pertinent data arrived from the Captain, Security Queen, or from Corporation headquarters.

As Mina's fingers danced across her keyboard, I couldn't help noticing the shocks from the laser torpedoes were becoming less intense. Suddenly the Captain's voice thundered through the navigation room. "Armed intruders aboard ship!"

Mina glanced at me just long enough to say, "They must've blown the docking bolts," then riveted her eyes to her screen. A minute later two solar hunks with sub-atomic projectile dispensers entered the room and commanded us to move away from our terminals. I looked at Mina. She shrugged, rose and moved into a corner.

I was following her when one of the solar hunks came right over to me, grabbed me by the arm and led me into the corridor.

My mind raced in fear. Would the solar hunk's radiation kill me, or would he destroy me with his weapon first? In either case I was doomed. With a choking sensation in my throat and my heart pounding like a lunar smelting pump, I walked in the direction he indicated, my destination and fate unknown.

*

I woke up, in my quarters, on my bed, feeling a little groggy. As my eyes opened, I recognized the place and remembered who I was. Then, like a flash of solar fire or the kick of deja vu, I recalled what had happened with the invader from Uranus.

First, he'd locked us in my room. Then, to my horror, he began to make love to me. I was terrified at first; the amount of radiation I was being exposed to would kill me in no time at all. But the solar hunk must have read my thoughts because he stopped and started talking to me. I presumed that he did not know Earthling, but had one of those instant translators built into his bandolier. The hunk sat on my bed. I watched his expressionless face, my eyes occasionally roving to take in his superb musculature as he began to speak.

"Bart," he began, "you will not die from the radiation."

I started to protest that I most surely would but he pressed on, refusing to allow me to speak.

"We are not your enemies! We have been ill-used by the crafty Kraveners. They are using us to get to your people. It's true they have mutated my people with their pellets of

59

unstability. But the radiation is not contagious! They have tried to make you believe a falsity and they have created many untruthful scenarios so that you would infer what they wanted you to believe. My fellow creature, we wish you no harm. In fact, I have been instructed to inform you that my people will not hold your people responsible for the raid you perpetrated on one of our ships. You were intentionally misinformed and misled. It is my mission to communicate these thoughts to you so that your resources may be joined with ours to defeat the evil Kraveners."

As I listened to the alien's words, something instinctively told me that he was being honest. I wanted to believe him. What he said made sense. We'd had no prior quarrel with the Uranians. It was only when the Kraveners had begun to pillage the galaxy, bringing death and destruction everywhere they went, that our troubles started with our former friends.

The solar hunk went on to explain that after he left me, I'd fall asleep. Meanwhile, he and his comrades would leave. Upon awakening it would be my task to convince Captain Pulsar that he should cease fire and have a conciliatory brunch with the leader of the solar hunks. This I agreed to do. But before he put me to sleep, he taught me a few things about Uranian love that I'd never experienced before in life or study.

*

I relayed the message I was told by my Uranian captor.

"It's true," said the Captain. "I received a memo from headquarters. The renegades from Kraven are responsible for all of the death and destruction to the Uranians."

We'd convened—the Executive Council—in the conference room. Lucille watched the Captain's lips, then shook her head in disbelief. The fingers of her right hand danced on her left palm, as though she were making a reminder to herself. Garcia just stared at the Captain, attempting to rearrange the furniture in his mind. He'd been told that the Uranians were our enemies. Now he had to create an entirely new mental context. Adam stood up and paced the length of the room—something he picked up from watching too many of those primitive Hollywood videos.

"And what of the radiation?" I asked, almost afraid to hear the answer. After all, just hours before I'd been exposed to a lethal dose. I could picture my life slipping away as I spoke.

"That, as well," said the Captain. "We were deceived. If you are struck by one of the Kraveners pellets, you will die in half-lives like the Uranians. But contact with a victim—even intimate contact—is harmless."

I was so overwhelmed by this news that I started to cry. Lucille came over and placed her hands on my shoulders, her cheek next to mine. She kissed me and her eyes told me not to worry.

"Damage to the ship was minimal," continued the Captain. "The docking bolts will be repaired in a matter of hours. There were no casualties to crew or interior. They simply wanted to have a heart-to-heart with you, Bart."

As Lucille seated herself, I wiped away my tears and looked at Captain Pulsar. "What's next?"

"We're going to connect Garcia with whoever's in charge of the Uranian's offense force. Perhaps our combined power will enable us to defeat the Kraveners."

Adam said, "Captain?"

"Yes?"

Adam stopped moving. "I think Bart and I should gather all of the data we can regarding skirmishes with the Kraveners. Perhaps we'll discover some salient point or flaw to target our attack."

"Good thinking, Adam."

We were dismissed.

I accompanied Adam to the ship's library. While scouring the tapes for possible clues, Adam suddenly locked the library door and led me behind the bank of terminals on the island in the center of the room.

"Have you found something?" I asked.

"Not yet," he said. "Just thought I'd ease your mind."

"About what?"

61

"Contamination."

He pulled me toward himself and deep-tongued my throat. "There," he said when he was finished. "If you were contaminated—which you weren't—now I am too—which I'm not."

"But you're mostly machine," I protested, "what have you got to be afraid of?"

"I'm just as susceptible as you are. And don't you forget it."

We continued to search through the many banks of data. Hours later we still hadn't made any significant discoveries. Finally, Adam suggested that we take a break and he invited me to his cabin for some fast sex.

I accepted.

I guess now is a good time to mention that I'm a poly, which means that my genetic distribution is multifarious and unreconstructed. Most people descended from humans have one basic skin tone from head to feet. And some of those tones are downright gorgeous. From the darkest gleaming black to the brightest white—with a million shades in between including brown, olive, copper, orange, red, yellow and gold. But a poly is spotted. We're piebald. There is a patch of brown on my left arm, some red on my chest; my face is mocha but my ass is silvery white. I'm not attracted to other polys. I like well-blended skin tones that don't vary much. Why anyone would go out of his or her way for a tryst with me is beyond my comprehension. I'm not complaining. I'm simply amazed that anyone would find me attractive when there are so many others whom I feel are so much more sexy than I.

I had a great time with Adam. He's very imaginative and can do some pretty remarkable things with his body. For one thing, he can fuck your butt and suck your cock at the same time. I tried to reciprocate with him, once, and nearly snapped my spine. But for him it requires no effort at all. Whenever we dock at a Corporation starbase for some D & D—Debriefing and Distraction—Adam is so busy making new liaisons, we never see him until it's time to depart for another mission.

*

Once we found out that it was the Kraveners who were responsible for the quarkbusting, everything changed. We had to re-think the entire situation. Suddenly, the solar hunks were no longer our enemies. And it was difficult to accept the Kraveners as quarkbusters. We'd been raised to believe that Uranians were bad guys and Kraveners good guys. Trying to change our attitudes became a paramount concern. It was a little like finding out that what we'd considered to be red was now blue and vice versa.

Quarkbusting had become one of the major problems in the galaxy. Everytime an astro-physicist bombarded a quark incorrectly it had an adverse effect on every other quark in the entire cosmic chain, thereby having an adverse effect on the stability of the universe. Since everyone these days is concerned about the future, the ecology of the universe is at the forefront of our collective consciousness.

We had no idea that the Uranians would not only turn out to be good folks, but that they were willing martyrs as well. It was with a sense of shock that I received my orders regarding the war on the Kraveners. According to the Captain's missive, the Uranian solar hunks had volunteered to deploy themselves as a diversionary force so that our attack platoon could score some crucial hits.

Once again I was assigned to assist Mina in the navigation sector. The Indigo was speeding toward a Kraven warship. It's sort of funny being in a starship during a space battle. Unless you're on the bridge or in the missile room, you have little sense of what's going on.

I kept my attention divided between my screen and Mina. After the solar hunks initiated their kamikaze run, we fired at the Kraven fleet, immediately knocking out three of their principal vessels. After that, the rest scattered and we had no trouble picking them off. A few escaped, but they would pose no threat with their mother ship reduced to space dust.

When the Executive Council convened in the conference

room, I felt a little sad. As Adam recounted the events of the day I began to feel a rising in my throat. I realized that the solar hunk who'd made love to me had died so that others in the galaxy might live. The enormity of his sacrifice overwhelmed me and I felt awful because I didn't even know his name or anything about him.

Captain Pulsar could see that I was not well, and after the meeting was adjourned, asked me to meet him in his stateroom.

Very proud of his Asian heritage, the Captain had decorated his room with vases, tapestries and screens, handed down in his family for eons of generations. I was admiring the delicate artistry, the subtle coloring, the sensitive construction of these antiques when the Captain, dressed in a loose silk kimono, came up behind me and placed his hands on my shoulders. I turned.

"I want you to take me, Bart, act the part of the conquering hero and penetrate me."

He didn't have to explain any further. The Captain had a wonderful attitude toward sex. One which I could be comfortable with. Everyone is free to do what he/she/it wants, but if somebody doesn't want you to do it to them you can't. So you don't always get whom you want but you never have to do it with anybody you don't want to do it with either. I think it's the best we all can expect considering that we're all individuals with our own personal tastes, desires and dislikes. It's fair. Some societies that I've heard about or read about, had some pretty weird ideas about all of this. I'm happy with things the way they are.

And there I was with the Captain and he wanted me to relieve him of all responsibility, to take control, to let him feel the strength and will of another. It's not very often that someone as attractive and powerful as the Captain desires this of me, so I willingly complied. I thought of my dead Uranian lover, and of how much I loved the Captain and I channeled these thoughts into aggressive sex. I fucked the Captain with all of the passion and force of which I was capable. It was incredibly satisfying. When it was over the

Captain smiled and sighed. I felt transcendent, like a transformation had occurred. There was a glow and a buzz that leapt from my body to my brain to my heart to my soul.

After the Corporation Mothers learned of our battle, they sent many congratulations. Not only for defeating the enemy, but for determining who was who. The Captain insisted that we hold a formal memorial ceremony for our slain Uranian brothers and sisters. It was a brief, simple, solemn gathering. I felt all weak inside and almost cried again. Lucille and Mina stood on either side of me, offering comfort. Afterward Lucille signed to me that I was a hero; that I'd helped immeasurably to defeat the evil marauders, that I should hold the dead solar hunk's love forever in my heart. I kissed her and hugged her, then she and Mina went off to be by themselves. Later on I heard that they'd organized a Centurian Tulip Grope.

Meanwhile, most of the male crew members gathered in the gym. We laid the tumbling and wrestling mats side by side and indulged ourselves in a wildly frenetic Alpha-Delta Clusterfuck. It was pretty sensational what with the high spirits and general energy level of all concerned. We fucked and sucked for hours, rested, and then began again. This helped to foster our sense of community and brotherhood. And it strengthened our emotional bonds, giving us the courage to face whatever might be waiting for us as we cruised the wild, mysterious ever-expanding universe.

CANDY HOLIDAYS

This year Daryl was not a wizard, a vampire, or a telephone booth. Elvin was not a hippie, a clown, or a refrigerator. They sat in their apartment in the Village while a parade passed by just below their windows. Tots dressed up like Teenage Mutant Ninja Turtles waddled by. And a hundred adolescent girls from Brooklyn and Queens in Madonna costumes. Couples from Jersey doing Elvi and Marilyns, Lucys, Rickys, Ethels and Freds. The streets were lined with blue barricades and blue policemen and policewomen, a gauntlet to guide the slowly moving crowd, whistling, shrieking, laughing.

Daryl lifted a candy corn from a ceramic bowl, bit off the white part, chewed, then the yellow, chewed, and then the orange. He swallowed. "So, what are we going to do tonight?" He said it to the air of the room, his eyes gazing at no particular spot, certainly not at Elvin, who lit another cigarette.

"Why is it always me who has to make all the decisions? Your turn."

"I don't know. I never know."

Daryl rose and turned on the television set, increasing the volume until the parade sounds were gone. Elvin lifted a magazine and turned pages.

Halloweens past had been miraculous. Ritualistic. Tiny seeds planted long ago in the marrow of their genes had finally burst forth in a splash of awesome color. The gray and brown of childhood uncertainty, the black and white of teenage angst had been supplanted by the freedom of adulthood. As a grownup you might have to spend a lot of time pulling weeds from the garden. But the occasional blooming, the sporadic wild party made everything worthwhile.

Daryl and Elvin arrived in New York, separately, about seven years ago. They've lived together for the past three. Halloween had been a highlight of their tandem journey through the city. But lately, forward motion had become difficult. The travelers had not been connecting with their usual agility and finesse. The very terrain, the ecosystem and infrastructure of their environment was in decay. More violence. More homeless. More disease. More litter. When Daryl got off the bus from Maine, when Elvin had flown in from Georgia, they perforated their edges to mesh with the city's gears. Eventually they bumped into each other, found that they could blend together with ease, soften for one another the brutal blows of surviving. But they'd somehow lost the formula, accidentally bent a working part out of shape, and now sat idly, letting their annual bacchanal slip by. Little boys like Daryl and Elvin had marked time in the prison of youth, weathering the tortures of traditional family oppression, eager and anxious to escape parents, siblings, small-town gossip, to go to a big city and sample the forbidden flavors denied them all their lives. The trips from Penobscot, Maine and Whispering Pines, Georgia to New York were necessary steps to move beyond stigmatized beginnings and claim the glamour of a wild flower, a strange breed in a queer brood in a large, throbbing, loud and crazy metropolis.

"We could go to a bar and drink," said Daryl, shaking a handful of candy corn like dice.

"We could go to a club and dance," said Elvin.

"Too crowded on Halloween. Coat check would take an hour."

"Bars would be crowded too."

"Maybe there's something good on the tube." Daryl threw back his head and popped the candy corn into his mouth, then picked up the remote and sifted through the images. Elvin gazed down at the magazine in his lap, started tapping his foot lightly, intertwining the nervous fingers that seemed to want to leap from his hands.

The room, dim with the blinds closed and only the reading lamp providing any light, shrank before Elvin's eyes. He closed them. Then glanced around. And noticed the shabbiness of the couch, the worn-out spots in the carpet. Certainly not the beautiful surroundings with brand-new expensive things he'd seen in magazines and had daydreamed about owning. But this was not the source of his unrest. The apartment—not the cause, but a symptom—merely reflected the tattered and unkempt relationship of its occupants. Elvin looked at the Jeff Stryker dildo, wound in a double helix of Mardi Gras beads, like a shrine, on the mantel. Somehow Daryl had become less accessible, less agreeable, not fun anymore, and Elvin, though he still loved him, wanted to get away. Not completely. But at least move out. Get his own apartment. Try to keep Daryl as a friend and lover, but jettison the roommate thing.

"We should do something," said Daryl. "It's our night of nights."

Elvin lit another cigarette. Looked at Daryl with a cool, even stare. Asked himself why he and this very attractive person in the armchair had become like two magnets, one facing the wrong direction, pushing away from one another. "I don't feel like going out. Everything'll be too crowded and noisy. My life is crazy enough."

Daryl turned off the television set. And sat down, heaving a sigh. What is it with you, he wanted to say. What the fuck's going on? Why can't we just get along anymore? But he said nothing. Words would lead to an argument that would end in nastiness and anger. He looked at Elvin with eyes that attempted to send up a white flag of truce.

Elvin looked at those eyes and saw nothing but insolence

and disgust. He tried to look neutral. Then stared down at the floor.

For several long minutes time became a rack upon which they were lashed at the wrists and ankles, stretching, stretching, with pain emanating from the heart to the limbs, burning, molten lava in every vein.

Daryl breathed deeply and very calmly, exceedingly gently said, "I need to go out. Come on. Let's try to have some fun."

Elvin let the magazine slide from his lap. Then bent to retrieve it and stood up in one swift movement. He yawned, said, "I think I'll take a nap. Go. Have a good time. Really. See you later." The words, the intonation, the inflection, weren't quite as he'd intended. Maybe it would be good for them to spend the evening apart. He'd tried to back down, see if a brief respite from each other might have a positive effect, but perhaps something undefinable from within had shaped the words to convey something else. When they were spoken Daryl heard them as sarcastic, challenging, a dare that could not go unacknowledged.

"Well. Fine. That's what I'll do. Right now." As he rose and his mind clicked into departure mode—jacket, keys, money—he could feel pressure, pushing his chest down, making him breathe faster, harder. He moved quickly, efficiently completing the circuit from the chair to the table to the coat stand, dropping the keys into his pocket, patting the other for his wallet, then, without a backward glance, opened the door and walked out.

Elvin watched the cute little buns pulsate away and then disappear, cute little buns attached to a manly body with an ever youthful face. He played a Sarah Vaughan album and flung himself onto the couch. He tried to listen to the music but his mind, not in the mood, bombarded him with images and impressions. Some felt good. Others pierced him like lances. The dream had not come true. Or, to be more accurate, it had come true but it didn't look like it was supposed to. He'd leave Georgia to go to New York. Become a famous dancer and choreographer. Fall madly in love. Live in a fabulous apartment. And all of this had occurred. But not quite. To Elvin it seemed a cruel joke. He'd come to New York as planned, but just when the serious decay began. The dance gigs were few and he worked part-time as an aerobics instructor. He loved Daryl but was not happy. And the apartment, never quite fabulous enough, was even less so now. It seemed like his life was going on inside of a funhouse mirror, the correct images reflected but strangely distorted, shapeless and confusing.

Cute little buns, he thought, and I'm not even interested anymore. For a moment he considered going out to trick. Then remembered how much he'd hated having to search for sex in sleazy places—truck stops back home, backrooms and dungeons in New York. The three seconds of divine, transcendent pleasure were always rewarding. But the weirdos, the furtiveness, the rapidity, the germs and other microorganisms passed around like canapes were not appetizing. He'd been grateful when he'd met Daryl. Felt like he'd been freed from the bondage of torture. And now he did not want to return.

Sarah Vaughan sang and Elvin paid no attention, listening to the voices in his head, telling him everything he did not want to hear.

In a bar, which he hadn't visited in two years, situated in the Village near the river, Daryl stood, looking, watching, taking in all the sights like a camera, seemingly unaware that he was attracting as much scrutiny as the guys he himself observed. Unaware of his own appearance and desirability, he would have been unimpressed if anyone had acknowledged his presence. Some men have to work hard to look their best. To others good looks come easily and there are those who, doted upon at a very young age, develop a conceit, spoiled because their admirers demand so little of them. But Daryl, keenly interested in everything going on around him, eager to try everything, wanted to experience all the amazements of the world. And thought seldomly of himself. In bars he'd always be surprised when anyone addressed him. It was like being jerked from the air and placed on the ground. As though he was completely unaware that he could be analyzed just as easily as everyone else in the room. But it didn't matter. Daryl would stutter through the compliments, thanking the stranger profusely, become embarrassed, and quickly turn the conversation around to inquiries, focusing the spotlight on the other.

It was one of the newer bars that had opened on the near side of the plague curve. When the disease had first been detected and hysteria had mounted to a vomiting volcano of despair, many businesses had closed. But though the virus had not yet been conquered, a gradual return to a more normal mood had resulted in some new enterprises. Off to the right were a few scattered tables, to the left the bar, separated by a long wooden divider, waist high. At the far right corner, a screen played porn videos, on the right, another ran music videos. Hip Hop rhythms, in sync with neither screen, played loudly.

Daryl bought a drink. Stood close to the front near the entrance and surveyed the room. If Elvin had been there he would have remarked that it seemed like a nice place, good crowd. He realized that he was alone and for a moment felt uncomfortable. He hadn't gone to a bar without Elvin in a long time. He hadn't cruised, with serious intent, since meeting Elvin. Out of practice, out of shape. But he eventually relaxed. Whatever happens, happens, he told himself. I'm just going to have a good time.

There were corporate executives dolled up in high drag with makeup and feathers and wigs and sequins and accessories, and school teachers and doctors in serious leather with caps and vests and handcuffs and boots, a few people masquerading as media celebrities, and a few, like Daryl, who wore standard, urban cruising attire.

A hand gripped his left butt cheek and he spasmed and giggled and turned to look at who had grabbed him. A man, somewhat taller, with a saggy face, slack lips and a bloated belly said, "Hi there. Happy Halloween. You know you're very cute."

Daryl blushed, said thank you, and asked the man about

his occupation, where he lived, are you a native New Yorker? He listened attentively, yet moved his eyes so they would not lock into the stranger's intense stare. Just when the man thought he might be making some progress, Daryl shook his hand, said it was nice talking to you, and walked away, sat down at an empty table and looked back and forth at the screens.

When a waiter came by and asked him if he wanted another drink, Daryl declined, then noticed a guy, pretty good-looking, watching him, smiling. He approached, grabbed the waiter by the arm and said, "Wait a second," then turned to Daryl and asked, "Can I buy you a drink?"

He nodded, said yes, the man sat down, they drank and talked, and when it came time to decide which apartment to go to, the question was quickly resolved.

The bed was large, the mattress hard, and Daryl enjoyed his nakedness upon it. An assortment of condoms, lubes, cock rings and dildos adorned the night table. The man, with large bones and dark coloring, was gentle and soft at first, nurturing, loving, then became rougher, tougher, sending Daryl into ecstatic transports of warm sensation. Each article of clothing he'd removed reminded him of the person at home. And before becoming completely lost to sensuous pleasure, each touch evoked past encounters, previous situations, many with Elvin, in which he'd reached new peaks of excitement, had felt so good he'd left his body and departed to some exquisite astral plane.

When they returned to themselves Daryl felt gratitude for the man who'd lifted him up so very high. And fought pangs of guilt when he thought of Elvin. The one who'd been a rock every time things became unsteady. The one who'd shared everything with him and overlooked his mistakes. Elvin meant so much to him, and he loved him, but Daryl felt that they could no longer communicate. He couldn't figure out exactly when it had gone wrong, or how they'd managed to slip away from one another. They never had sex anymore. Hardly talked. Snapped at one another when they did. Never cuddled in bed. When was the last time they'd kissed?

He politely left the man, put on his clothing and told himself that when he arrived home he'd tell Elvin everything that had happened, all the thoughts that had lit up in his mind. They'd start communicating again and this would lead to a new, happier era in their lives.

Elvin had fallen asleep on the couch. When Daryl got home, at about 2:30 in the morning, he closed the door and moved about stealthily, removing his jacket and shoes, gently, silently, placing his keys and pocket money on the table. Too adrenalized to sleep, he sat in the armchair, eating candy corn in small sections, one tiny bite at a time. Elvin's gaunt face was beginning to show signs of age, tiny lines, a bit too much tanning. But Daryl was pleased to note that his lover's long, sinewy dancer's limbs, flat tummy and small waist, were still capable of making him want to reach out and touch. But this was not the time for sentimentality. Determined to vent his thoughts before he changed his mind and backed down, Daryl softly called out Elvin's name, attempting to awaken him without startling him. Elvin sighed, opened his eyes, immediately noted the awkward posture he'd melted into, and quickly sat up, rubbing his eyes, suppressing gap-mouthed yawns. "Must've fallen asleep," he mumbled.

"I'm sorry I woke you," said Daryl, "but I did a lot of thinking tonight and I think we should really have a serious talk. Now."

"About what?"

"About us."

"What about us?" Elvin could not help noticing that Daryl's hair looked slept upon, his pretty lips had that dry, chapped look, typical after sexual play involving the mouth, that his pants were not zipped up all the way.

"About us not getting along very well lately. We need to talk and figure out what the problems are, try to solve them."

"We should have talked before you decided to go out and play trick or treat with strangers."

Daryl flushed. He could never hide anything from Elvin. But what had given him away? Was it something I said, he

74

wondered, or maybe just the way I said it? "I won't lie to you," he said humbly. "Yes, I fooled around. But it made me realize how much I love you."

"Right," said Elvin, a roiling head of steam inflating his anger, "you love me so much that you decided to go out and contract the virus so that we could die horrible, premature deaths!"

Daryl was so shocked at these words it felt like his heart had stopped beating. "I swear," he sputtered, "we didn't exchange any bodily fluids we simply—"

"I don't want to hear about it!" Elvin cut him off, rising, moving toward the bedroom. "I'm sick of you, I'm sick of this apartment, I'm sick of this city, I'm sick of my life! And nothing you can say will change anything!"

*

Daryl, after two days in Penobscot with his family, finally reached the point where he wanted to be back in New York. Coming home for Christmas was always exciting. Temporarily. Then boredom and restlessness would fight for dominance in his thoughts, he'd become edgy and brusque, distracted, tired from the deception, the subterfuge, the game he'd have to play to simply spend time with his family. He sat on the worn-out couch before the fireplace in the living room with threadbare carpeting. Unlike Elvin, Daryl's family were very relaxed about such things— chipped coffee mugs and cigarette burns didn't bother them unduly—and Daryl had never been able to fully understand Elvin's obsession, his fastidiousness—downright pedantic, annoying—when it came to furnishings and the care thereof. But it didn't matter anymore. As Daryl had told his sister, Denise, the only member of his family who knew about his relationship with Elvin, the first evening home when she'd taken him into her room, closed the door and asked him how things were going.

"I moved out," he told her. "Haven't told Mom or Dad or Aunt Belle yet. I figure I'll tell them before I go back. Make up some excuse about how the building was condemned or something. I can tell them anything; they don't care."

"What happened!?!" she'd asked, reacting as though something catastrophic could be the only reason why two people living together for three years would break up.

Daryl was quick to reassure her that there had been no particular incident, nothing specific that could bear the blame, just a gradual shifting, an unidentifiable set of factors that resulted in a new equation. "Really," he told her, imploring her to accept his story, "I'm happier now. We weren't getting along and I tried to make things work but they didn't and everything's much better now." For a moment he considered telling her about his infidelity but decided against it.

Denise looked at him—all solicitude—and patted his shoulder. "I want you to have the best Christmas ever. It's too bad we can't tell anyone else what's happened. Dad and Aunt Belle might go a little easier on you if they knew you'd just gone through a serious, emotional, traumatic experience."

Daryl wanted to reach out, pull her toward himself, wrap his arms around her and cry on her shoulder, tell her, yes, you've got it exactly, it was serious, emotional and traumatic. But he forced a smile, raised his hand in a gesture meant to convey sincerity, and assured her that he was fine, everything had worked out for the best in this best of all possible worlds.

"If I told the family I'm queer things would be a lot worse than they are right now, that's for sure."

"They know. They just don't want to talk about it." Denise scowled, "I hate that word—queer. When I hear people use it at work it makes me so mad."

"In New York that's what we call ourselves now. Gay is obsolete."

"Really," she exclaimed, brightening, "it's so hard for us country bumpkins to stay up-to-date with you fast-movin' city folk."

They laughed. And talked about Denise's boyfriend, Carl, whom she'd been dating for several years and everyone assumed she would eventually marry.

Daryl spent his mornings chatting with Mom in the kitchen, with his brother Donald in the bedroom they'd shared while growing up, with Dad in his workshop in the basement. They talked about the weather, TV shows, the lawn and the neighbors. Donald's wife, Megan, and their daughter, Tanya, six years old, were usually in the guest bedroom, watching TV, dressing and undressing Tanya's dolls. Daryl had little to say to them and tended to pass them by as he made his rounds.

After lunch he'd borrow someone's car and drive around, into the center of town, out to the quarries where he'd sunbathed nude on a flat rock, then to the steep, winding roads that led to the foothills where he'd sneaked cigarettes and beer with his pals. In the evenings he'd call local friends to see if they'd returned home for the holidays, he'd watch television with the family. Then late at night when they were asleep, he'd revolve and shudder in bed, wanting desperately to talk to someone in New York, but there was no one he could call. Steve, Jerry and Bennett would all be out of town visiting their families. Elvin was out of the question. He wished he could speak to Jim, Enrique or Mark, but since they'd died he found it too painful to even think about them. Daryl would finally drift into a restless sleep, in the mornings feel slightly out of it. Although the excitement of Christmas was building fast all around him, he wished he was back in New York, in the tiny apartment he'd found after leaving Elvin.

Mom busied herself with turkey, ham and fixings, Aunt Belle was responsible for soups, salads, vegetables, Denise baked cookies and pies, Dad erected the tree and decorated it with ornaments that had been in the family for generations and only he was allowed to handle, Donald did the exterior decorating with plastic carolers that lit up, wreaths, flashing lights and a weather-proof nativity diorama. Daryl, the youngest, and of whom the least was expected, would listlessly help out here and there, attempting to capture the family spirit, but not succeeding, wanting to be elsewhere doing other things. He could not say, exactly, what these other things were, but he knew, for certain, that he'd find them eventually.

When his father and brother argued about the impending war in the Persian Gulf, Daryl feigned interest but soon found his mind wandering. When they briefly stopped shouting at one another and asked Daryl his opinion, he confessed that he hadn't been paying attention and had to be reminded what they were talking about. "I haven't had much time to think about it," he told them and they wondered to themselves how he could be so uninterested and so uninteresting.

He belonged here, but he didn't fit in. Although his chromosomes bore the imprints of his mother's and father's blueprints, this cozily shabby gingerbread house in the game of Life was not nearly merry enough for Christmas, for him. He felt like an alien who'd been planted in his mother's womb. He could talk to Denise. But the rest of them were like strangers. Even the ribbon candy that Mom would buy and set out on a folding tray near the tree each year didn't taste right anymore. The reds were not cherryish enough, the yellows not lemony.

It was the gap, he finally realized, as he'd circle away from Aunt Belle every time she came near. The gap that existed between Daryl's truth and the family's denial. Except for Denise, the only bridge, who bore the weight of her brother's dilemma.

Aunt Belle, his father's older sister, was the glue that held the family together, the sandpaper who wore everyone out. She was short and round, puffy-looking all over, her face like a dollop of mashed potatoes with the eyes and mouth scooped and filled with gravy. Attempting to keep things smooth, ultra-smooth, she bullied, manipulated, cajoled, withheld information, distorted facts. She made certain that everyone stayed in touch, got together often, ruddered the family ship through rough waters.

It was at a Christmas supper, back when Daryl was about eight years old, that Aunt Belle had inadvertently stopped the conversation at the table, changing the delicate family balance. Daryl had risen to fetch the salt and pepper and returned. She watched him move to and from the table, then turned to her brother and said, "Light on his feet, isn't he?"

It was as though everyone at the table was a marionette on strings jerked by unseen hands. They stopped eating. All eyes locked onto Daryl's father. He looked at his sister in shock, speechless. Belle offered her brother a tender look that meant to say, I'm sorry, but it was too late to take back the words and pretend they hadn't been uttered. For a prickly second all eyes scanned around the table, avoiding Daryl's eyes, then everyone looked down at their plates and continued eating.

Since that moment, years ago, the subject of Daryl's gait has not been broached, except between Daryl and Denise. Aunt Belle, the navigator, would pinpoint reefs and shallows, smoothly maneuvering away from any potential danger zones. Should the subject of marriage arise, for instance, she would dominate the conversation, offering explicit instructions for Denise and Donald, but, then, changing themes, speak of Daryl's attributes and his potential to excel in any field he might choose. If the conversation should veer too closely to the exact details of her nephew's living arrangements in New York City, Aunt Belle would, in a mock-complicitous, winking manner imply that Daryl's roommate—if in fact he had one—is a private concern that no one should discuss or question, then alter the flow, praising the cultural plenitude and delightfully cosmopolitan nature of his new home.

Loving her for her concern, but hating her for creating this knot of silence that nothing could unravel, the worst of it, her overprotectiveness, always came after every Christmas supper when she would insist that he sit with her and they talk. A very one-sided conversation in which she would ask him if he still had that low-paying job, what-do-you-call-it, not for profit?

"Yes," he'd say, firmly, "I'm still working at the Lytton Foundation."

"That's the, uh, not for profit thing?" she'd ask, a slightly sarcastic tone creeping from her mouth.

"Yes."

"Well, Daryl, dear, you'll just have to explain it to me one more time. How can anything be not for profit? And how can you make a decent living at it?"

He'd explain to her the grants he administered that went to scholars, artists, hospices, day care centers, but she would cut him off and lecture without mercy about the cold hard facts of life, and nice guys finishing last and fat bank accounts and the survival of the fittest.

Daryl would want to shake her and tell her that he was happy with his work, thrilled with his life, deliriously in love with a wonderful man, but he sat there, pretending to heed her, mentally contradicting every word.

And this year's conversation with Aunt Belle would be worse than usual. Because this year he didn't have a wonderful man to hold as a prize in his thoughts. So, after supper, after he'd helped clear the table, when Aunt Belle attempted to corner him in the living room, he snuck downstairs to his father's workshop, where Dad and Donald would go to escape from the women, sat on a plastic milk crate near the bandsaw, listening to them argue about the arms buildup, the troops deployed, the financial factors and environmental considerations. He listened, offered his opinions, trying desperately not to think about Aunt Belle, Christmas, New York, his tiny new apartment or Elvin.

*

It was the loneliest, quietest, saddest Valentine's Day Elvin had ever known. He sat on the new couch, staring at the new carpeting, Christmas gifts to himself. He thought that getting some new things, rearranging the furniture a bit, would help him adjust to life without Daryl. And also, since he had nowhere to go for Christmas, that it might cheer him up as he sat by himself while the rest of the world celebrated mightily. He could have visited people for the holidays, taken the money spent on the apartment and gone traveling for a while instead. But there was no one he wished to visit in Whispering Pines, Georgia. When he'd been caught behind the filling station with a trucker from Alabama, word had spread through town like wildfire. And when his adoptive parents had said goodbye the day after he graduated from high school, they told him that the best way he could repay their generosity, the huge debt he owed them, was never to have any contact with them whatsoever, never again. He would not miss them. He'd learned not to love them. They fed him, clothed him and sent him to school. But that was all. That was all. That was all.

He could have visited Charlie in San Francisco or Sherry in L.A., ex-dance partners whom he'd speak with on the phone a few times a year. But Charlie had recently moved in with someone and Elvin would make the situation lopsided, the third, unnecessary wheel. Sherry and her husband and kids would be too sweet for words; they'd throw him into a deep depression as he would torture himself with cruel memories of his childhood, regretting everything, wishing he'd grown up elsewhere. And there was no one to hang out with here. Manhattan had simply become a graveyard. Over the past six years Elvin had lost eleven friends—three dancers, two musicians, two composers, a director, an actress, an ex-lover who'd become a good friend, and the guy who used to live next door who would look after Elvin's apartment when he was on tour as Elvin would do for him when he was on vacation.

Christmas had been awful. He'd gotten used to Daryl's annual trek to Maine every winter, but this year had been worse—there was no joyful return to anticipate now. On the most romantic day of the year, Elvin had only his new carpet and new couch for companionship.

Until the phone rang.

"Elvin, this is Paul."

He had to think for a moment. Who's Paul?

"Paul Bergman. I teach the aerobics class following yours?"

"Right. Hi, Paul. What a surprise. How are you?"

"Fine. Fine. You?"

"Great. Just…terrific."

"The reason I called is, well, you probably have other plans but just in case you don't—and I hope this doesn't sound too crass or corny—but you're recently divorced and I'm recently widowed and I thought—why don't we get together and see if we can have a good time. You know, just friendly-like. Dinner, maybe a movie or something, then split. What do you think? Don't be afraid to say no, I can handle it."

Elvin didn't know what to say at first. This possibility had never appeared in his mind; he did not think that he'd ever get any closer to the other aerobics instructor than the briefest of greetings when they passed at the gym. And he figured he'd be spending the evening alone with his books and records. If this had been planned, if they'd made arrangements beforehand, by now Elvin would have thought of a hundred reasons why he shouldn't go through with it. Would have come up with some very plausible excuses to bow out. But having had no time to consider all the angles, and allowing for the possibility that this might be fun, he blurted, "Well, I think this is a great idea. I had no plans, really. It would be nice. Tell me where and when and I'll be there."

Elvin had entered a state of limbo, had ceased to feel any of the intensity of life since Daryl had moved out. The comforting solidity of things had given way to ground-rumbling instability, the threat that all support could crumble at any second, that he'd been overtaken by a void of isolation which threatened to turn him into a hysterical madman. The offer from Paul was the first sign he'd seen in quite some time that life could still hold pleasant surprises in store for the unsuspecting. And by the end of the evening, before he walked home, Elvin managed to piece together a vague picture of what he wanted; he'd finally broken through a thin, wet membrane and found what he wanted on the other side.

He stood in the back of the backroom club where Paul had taken him, after a late dinner at a French restaurant. Elvin could hear the slurping and groaning sounds, zippers opening and closing, sighs and whispers from the creatures cavorting in the dark. He thought back on his conversation at the restaurant with Paul. Colette's had just opened several months ago. Paul had raved about it. Elvin hadn't been there, hadn't been to any new anythings since he'd started spending time with Daryl. Once they'd found a good Chinese restaurant, or a friendly bar where they could meet after work, they would rarely try any other, figuring why keep searching after you've found something that works well for you? Safe. Dull. And as Elvin sat in the warm and comfortable, nice but not pretentious atmosphere of the restaurant, enjoying escargots, duck, wine, he realized that this is what had happened to his wonderful journey with Daryl. They'd been trudging down the same roads day after day, at work, at play—particularly in bed—and they'd simply become bored with the same old routine.

Which is why Elvin was so agreeable, after they'd eaten and walked for a while in the chilly February windy air, almost eager to go to a backroom club that Paul had suggested. In the front, a juice bar with video games, pinball machines, a pool table, a jukebox, and a crush of men passing into and out of a dark passage. Paul had plunged into the black maw while Elvin hung out at the bar for a while, considering whether to go any further. This furtive, anonymous, sex-in-the-shadows thing was what he'd told himself he'd hated more than almost anything. And who would risk any kind of harmful behavior with all of those fatal microbes everywhere? But, he convinced himself, he could dip his toes in, splash around a little, he didn't have to dive in headfirst. He could touch and fondle, be touched and fondled—even get naked if he wanted to—with no further obligation. There was no rulebook which said that he had to do this, this, or that as a requisite for permission to depart. He could just listen and sniff and watch if he wanted to. So, with his shoulders back and his tummy tight, he passed through the corridor that led to darkness.

It was like a funhouse, a mysterious interior with nooks and crannies formed by groups of bodies in differing configurations. As his eyes slowly became aware of shapely presences he moved into an empty corner, two men beside him, one standing upright, one on his knees. When Elvin had relaxed into the sturdy confluence of two concrete walls, allowed his physical and psychic weight to slip away, he sighed and a flow of warm sensation began to tickle him all over. When the man on his knees lifted his hand to Elvin's crotch and started manipulating his cock and balls through supple denim, Elvin looked down at the man's face lunging against the other man's crotch and felt himself responding, clicking into a steady vibration that escalated in speed and intensity until he rocked back and forth with the motion and finally fell back against the wall, unloading the pulsating tension that had built up in his groin. He caught his breath, moved as though in a daze, exited the room and hit the sidewalk, the cold bracing air, heading home, hearing echoes of words that Paul had said to him at dinner. When the conversation had skirted too closely to the subject of Elvin's ex-lover and Paul's deceased lover, they'd cautiously, delicately, exchanged thoughts and offered assuring comments, making this exchange, which had the potential for disaster, a comforting and uplifting commiseration of two lonely souls. Elvin thought that Paul was dealing remarkably well with his tragic loss, felt that he was someone he could confide in. So he opened his heart about the breakup with Daryl and when Paul had listened and said, "If I were you I'd buy him a heart-shaped box of chocolates and try to win him back," Elvin thought that maybe this wasn't such a bad idea.

*

At a small desk in the living room, Daryl sat and paged through a thin newspaper, pausing occasionally to read or skim an article. There was a stack of thin newspapers off to one side and a scissors on the other, a small pile of articles that had been clipped, several strips of marginal paper carelessly strewn. The apartment, nicely situated on the fourth floor, due to its corner location, offered sun—when it cared to shine—in the morning and in the afternoon. Finding it was a lucky break, the cost not as high as some landlords would have had it. A sunny Sunday morning, Daryl's stacks of paper rose and fell, he felt contented, well-rested, and suddenly thinking it too quiet, reached to turn on the radio, lowering the volume to a softer level.

Elvin was the one who'd taught Daryl everything he knew about music, which wasn't much, but Daryl was grateful for the instruction. Unlike Elvin whose knowledge of music was vast, who could sing and play the piano, Daryl was the kind of American boy who didn't go to rock concerts and never owned a guitar, hadn't shown any interest in theater or opera, cringed at the suggestion of piano lessons or the church choir. He could rarely recall song titles and had trouble identifying the names of vocalists and groups. During the disco years there were songs he danced to hundreds of times which he could not name if the fate of the universe depended on it.

Daryl's awareness of how much he'd learned from Elvin deepened, broadened, and he'd begun to think of ways, subtle, small ways, to say thank you. Elvin brought a certain intensity to his life. Things were never quite as surprising and exciting when Elvin wasn't around. Alone, Daryl felt unplugged, unconnected in the dark. When they were together it was like being part of an electrical circuit with tingling currents zipping from fingers to toes and back, everything for your ears glorious and fascinating, everything for your eyes a wonderment of dazzling color and light.

Elvin slept late, almost reaching consciousness, then sliding back into nowhere, finally awakening, shifting onto his back, his hands clasped behind his head, looking, coming back into focus. His arms ached a bit, unlike his legs, unused to the workouts he'd had lately. But it felt good. He was in the best shape he'd ever been which made the first signs of aging—his hair thinning and receding, skin lined and leathery—somewhat easier to handle. When he'd finally taken an unflinching, realistic look at his life he knew that he would not be able to dance and teach aerobics forever. He'd joined Paul, taking a course in physical therapy, an occupation that appealed to him more with time and experience. He and Paul had become rather chummy, meeting every so often for drinks or dinner, chatting a bit before and after classes. When Paul would ask Elvin if he wanted to go to a sex club, he declined. Eventually he stopped asking. Neither had any family in New York. Both had lost numerous friends and acquaintances. It's a miracle, Elvin thought, that just when I really needed a friend, there he was. Feeling confident and centered finally, after such a protracted period of uncertainty, Elvin thought about breakfast. Or maybe brunch. Whatever.

Like the pieces of a puzzle falling naturally into place, Elvin and Daryl had overcome their previous mistakes. If they'd thought the picture had a few things wrong with it after living together for three years, it had seemed completely undecipherable after they'd split up. But like salmon who follow the dictates of their genetic code and fight the brutal currents to return to their place of birth, so too had Daryl and Elvin, first following the beacon that beckoned from New York, then following their hearts when they realized how much they'd lost by separating. Though things might not be perfect, at least there was something to hold onto, another person to share the tragedies and the miracles. Elvin, for the first time ever, felt a sense of security and continuity. To Daryl it looked like a gray film or dullness had been rinsed from his eyes, the world now much brighter and more colorful, vivid in ways it had never been before.

Daryl finished clipping, then sorted the articles into three piles, articles about gay legislation, gay bashing, gay outing, gay artists, gay policemen, gay soldiers, placed them in envelopes addressed to Mom, Dad and Aunt Belle. Then, cleaning up the mess, felt jabs of hunger and wandered into the kitchen. But instead of eating anything, he decided to wait for Elvin to wake up and scoured, rinsed and dried all the dishes from last night. Then sat on the couch, the new one Elvin had bought, the color of which—maroon—Daryl was not too crazy about, but, he had to admit, looked classier than the old one. First he ate some jellybeans from the candy dish, carefully avoiding the greens and blacks. Then, went to the refrigerator and got a few red, gold, silver and blue foil-covered chocolate eggs, returned to the couch and let them, one by one, melt slowly into his tongue.

The argument started after they'd finished eating, but the seeds were planted when Elvin finally emerged from the bedroom, greeted Daryl with a kiss, asked him if he was ready to go to brunch, and Daryl, having waited for so long became a mite testy and countered the idea with the suggestion that instead they go to lunch. Elvin wanted to know what the difference was. "You can order anything you like anywhere we go," he said.

When they sat at the small table in the omelette-waffle-ice cream emporium, and ate eggs Benedict, sipping Bloody Mary's, hardly a word was exchanged. They walked to the pier and sat in the breezy sunshine. Gazing at people passing by and at the Jersey shore across the water, they sat on a concrete ledge, in silence, until Elvin decided to try to break through the barrier, the thin walls of the twin bubbles that surrounded them, by asking Daryl what he thought of the film they'd seen last night. Atypically, they hadn't discussed it immediately after because the phone rang as the credits rolled and Elvin had talked while Daryl went to bed. Daryl praised the writing and the story but didn't care for the acting or directing. Elvin, dumbfounded, usually in agreement with Daryl about these things, voiced a differing opinion. They argued, calmly, reserved, each trying to cling to the top wrung, maintaining the cool, detached tone of he who is right. When Daryl said, "The only good thing about it was that it's politically correct," Elvin, exasperated, blurted, "You're getting so goddamned political lately. Lighten up!"

"Well, maybe I am. Maybe you should be getting more political too!"

The rhythm, the velocity of their interchange stopped short, then began again in a new mode, one that was easier, softer. Elvin looked at Daryl's eyes with humility in his own, placed his hand on Daryl's knee and said, "Maybe you're right."

They came together again, blending smoothly, creamily, finding things to laugh about as they walked back to the apartment, the sidewalks and streets still festooned with plastic leprechaun hats, beer cans, strips of green and yellow ribbon, shattered whiskey bottles, a tattered, rain-streaked sign that said NO FAGGOTS IN IRELAND and another that read IRISH QUEER. Back home, they listened to the messages on the answering machine. One was from Charlie, Elvin's friend in San Francisco, wanting to share the news that his cousin who'd been sent to the Persian Gulf was on his way back, safe and sound. Then, a message from Aunt Belle, wishing Daryl and his friend a happy Easter—and, by the way, what's with all these newspaper clippings? And finally, Paul, asking if Elvin and Daryl would like to go dancing later that evening.

"You wanna go dancin'?" Elvin asked, a leering grin on his face.

"Let's dance," said Daryl, picking up some jellybeans, tossing one at Elvin, who scooped some from the dish, popped one in his mouth and lobbed a couple at Daryl. Chuckling, they pelted each other, with handfuls eventually, a confetti rainbow of soft pellets flying and falling, then laughed themselves silly on the couch, tumbling into a tight embrace, heat growing between them, two horny Easter bunnies cuddling in a celebration of life.

LUBRICITY

Shafts of light and glowing dots gliding around. Out of shadows and dark crevices in the air, bullets of brightness slipped through the mists, illuminating patches all around me. I was still in my room, I think. But in a strange sector of time and space: different dimension, another reality. Floating and unfettered. Sliding about in a jarful of wet, warm satin. I had the sensation of containment, yet I was unbound. Nothing looked normal and my eyes were captivated by the vapors, the shadows, the trails and auras of light.

Earlier, I had been reading. Then I watched a video. And eventually, read some more. My room disappeared. I swirled in a vortex of Spanish moss and kaleidoscopic color. From out of nothing tactile, figures emerged. An elderly gentleman with hollow cheeks and sad eyes. He appeared to be seated on a large, ornate throne. As he hove into view I could see that he sat opposite another gentleman—middle-aged with tanned skin and a thoughtful countenance. The second man's chair seemed ordinary to me, modern and unexceptional. Between the two men, a three-tiered chess board floated above a squat plinth.

They maneuvered amethyst knights, onyx rooks, acquamarine pawns and they talked. The younger would describe the buttocks or genitals of a sensuous youth and the elder would smile and nod in agreement. The elder would relate a somewhat brutal tale, smirking. I realized who these men were. Are. For earlier that evening I had been reading *The 120 Days Of Sodom*, after having watched several scenes of the videocassette. Shortly before these visions entered my room, or I was transported to a bizarre reality zone, I had placed the book and the videocassette—one atop the other—on my table. Had the union of these two objects somehow engendered this fantastical manifestation? I was as uncertain then as I am now.

The Marquis noticed me first and summoned me closer with his gnarled index finger. "You may watch," he said, leering.

Pasolini took notice of me, "...and listen," he added, then returned his attention to the chess set.

From behind me, as if on an invisible hovercraft, a heavyset man drifted into view. He leaned over and offered to shake my hand. Grasping his plump fingers I started to introduce myself. Before I could manage a syllable he said, "Phil, Phil K. Dick. PKD. Pleased to meet you."

I recalled that the day before I had finished reading Ubik.

The darting lights and wavering veils—lavender, lime, crimson, cerulean—settled and slowed a bit as the game proceeded. The Marquis and Pasolini were transfixed by the small figures before them.

PKD and I watched, rapt, in silence. I could hear the gentle clang of platinum bells and inhaled the scent of oranges and cloves.

This must be heaven. Or hell for divine sinners, I thought.

"Heaven!" scoffed the Marquis.

"Heaven and hell are one and the same," said Pasolini.

PKD grinned.

The game resumed. But I had to interrupt. I could not stop myself. "Is this some sort of punishment?" I asked.

The Marquis looked up and Pasolini turned his head to face me.

"I mean, do you suffer much?"

"Constantly," said Pasolini.

The Marquis chuckled. "In suffering there is pleasure—in pleasure is suffering."

PKD smiled, as though very pleased.

I couldn't let this precious moment go to waste. I gathered my resolve and plunged ahead. "Why did they persecute you?"

The Marquis shook his head, as though in disbelief. "For daring to tell the truth and rub their pretty faces in it."

"Ah, yes," Pasolini agreed, "the truth."

PKD sighed, "There are so many truths." And then he almost faded from sight. But reappeared a moment later. I wondered if this was to be my fate. Would I spend eternity with these three? If so, what had I done to merit their company? I have accomplished nothing to compare to the man who viewed sex through a prism; the man who conquered beautiful and the ugly with his unflinching eyes; the man who balanced on the point where multiple perspectives intersect.

Faced with the possibility, I wanted to stay with these three. They would educate and amuse me, massage my mind.

But as these thoughts visited I could feel myself sliding away. Slipping into familiar mundanity. The lights were fading, the bells more distant, the incense became faint.

I realized that this could be the end. "And what of passion?" I cried.

PKD chortled.

Pasolini smiled.

The Marquis sneered.

"Not the object," I protested as the vision rolled away, "the method!"

"Passion is humiliation," quipped the Marquis.

"Passion is politics," countered Pasolini.

"Passion is individual, transient, and multifarious," insisted PKD.

And then they were gone. I was alone on my bed. Reclining

like an odalisque. I glanced around. At the stacks of books, cassettes, discs. And eventually melted into a long, dreamless sleep.

BOYS IN THE SAND

The President paces back and forth, sand beneath his shoes, in a large tent in the desert. He is in Saudi Arabia to negotiate a peace settlement. The entire world waits anxiously. Barbara, The First Lady, did not accompany the President, opting instead to remain in Washington to teach the alphabet to Dan Quale.

It's a warm night in the desert and an Arab boy, aged twelve, waving large paper fans, flutters about the President, cooling his torpid brow.

"Can't you do that any faster, for gosh sakes?" he pouts petulantly. "In the great states of America we have something called air conditioning."

The boy does not respond, either with gesture or sound. When the President is not looking at him he crosses his eyes and sticks out his tongue.

"Gosh darn it, I'm lonely," says the President. "I wish they could have taught this poor unfortunate waif some English so I'd at least have someone to talk to."

The waiting makes him uneasy. He glances at his Rolex and sighs.

Just then, the flaps of the tent part and the President's secret envoy for Operation Desert Oblivion enters.

"How the fuck are ya, Georgie?" says Roseanne.

"You're finally here!" he clasps his hands in gratitude. "Gosh darn it, now we can begin!" The President grins and says to himself, 'If Saddam Hussein has any kind of dick at all, the person to shrivel it down to size is Roseanne Barr!' He rubs his hands gleefully.

"Let's get this friggin' show on the road," she chirps. "Ya got your secret weapons handy, Georgie Porgie?"

The President beams, "Present and accounted for." He clears his throat, claps his hands and loudly says, "Gentlemen!"

The flap at the other end of the tent swings inward and two men, maximum muscle, wearing jogging pants and tanktops, enter and stand at attention.

A tear wells in the President's right eye. "Roseanne, in case you haven't already met them, I'd like to introduce you to my dear friends. Sly Stallone and Arnie Schwarzenegger. Gosh darn it, I'll say it—America's finest!"

"Hey guys," she hails, "yo, how's it hangin'?"

Arnie smiles and says, "Vell, I think it be just fine."

Sly grins and says, "Duh, I'm ready and rarin' to go."

Roseanne places her hands on her hips. "Okay, boys, let's see what ya got."

The President looks at Arnie. Arnie looks at Sly. Sly looks at the President. All three look at Roseanne.

"You mean, here? Now?" sputters the President.

"Of course!" snaps Roseanne. "I gotta see what my fuckin' bargaining power is, don't I?"

The President dismisses the Arab boy, lowers his hands, squares his shoulders and salutes. "I guess it's time to get down to business, gentlemen."

"Vell," says Arnie, "I guess if ve must and ve have to, den ve vill."

Sly says, "Duh, yeah."

"Okay, Gorgeous Georgie," says Roseanne, "you go first."

"This is for God and my country and, of course, Barbara back home," says the President as he unzips his pants.

'Poor Barbara,' is Roseanne's first thought.

The Arab boy raises his hand to his mouth, hiding a grin.

94

"Dis is for de great American economy, and God and country too you best belif it, and especially for Hollyvood, my new home," says Arnie as he pulls down his pants.

'Uh oh,' says Roseanne to herself, 'strike two.'

The Arab boy raises his other hand to his mouth, the balls of his feet pivoting in the sand.

Sly pulls down his pants, says, "Duh, yeah, what dese guys just said."

Roseanne crosses her arms over her chest. "Well, I guess we really are in a recession! But what the fuck, I'll give it my best shot."

The President's eyebrows converge as he says, "We can do better than this! Gosh darn it, I know we can!"

He starts stroking himself, but not seeing any improvement, looks toward the corner for some assistance from the Arab boy, who just a moment before crawled out of the tent and disappeared into the night.

The President looks at his dear friend, Arnie.

"Vell," he says, "I'm a patriot and I vill do my best."

He gets to his knees and sucks the President's cock. There is no apparent change in length or diameter.

"Duh, maybe you're doing it wrong," says Sly, bending over to get a closer look.

Just then a SCUD missile tears through the roof of the tent, the pointy nose lodging in Sly's asshole, his jogging pants in smoking tatters at his feet. "Ouch," he says, glancing over his shoulder. "Hey, Mr. President, do you think this thing is loaded?"

The President pushes Arnie's face from his crotch and says, "Gosh. To tell you the truth we don't know very much about these particular weapons, military intelligence being what it is these days."

Roseanne looks askance, shakes her head in dismay and pushes out the flaps, exiting, shouting, "You guys are pathetic! I give up! This is a job for Roger Ailes!"

She commandeers a waiting jeep, guns the engine and roars into the night leaving a turbulent sand storm in her wake.

EXCERPT FROM
TRANSCRIPTION NO. 910524-103

[DELETE:]
Again? Are you serious? I've told you over and over. I didn't
do it. I swear...Oh. Okay. All right. Really. Just don't hit me
again, okay? I'm innocent. I swear. Really. Like I told you.
The first time I did it I met this guy who said his name was
Leon. You know? I was just driving by the pier, real slow, I
knew what I wanted but I'd never done it before. And so he
gets into the car and I, you know, did it and then paid him
and that was it. But then the fourth, or maybe the third time
it was Leon again. And he remembered me and I remembered him. So this time when it's over he tells me that I can
have a phone number and call him and he'll set me up with
all the young ones I want. You know? Avoid the possibility
of picking up someone who turns out to be an undercover
cop or a serial murderer or something. So I took the number.
And whenever I called to make an appointment either Leon
shows up or someone just like him. You know. Young, black,
willing. I don't know why it is that I'm so drawn to the
dark-skinned ones so much. I just know they excite me the
most. You know? So everything is great. I call once or twice
a week and the guys show up at any place I want and there's
no trouble. You gotta believe me when I tell you it was ideal.

I was never happier and less grouchy at work. It was the first time I was able to get my rocks off on a regular basis. I thought I never had it so good. But, anyway, that's how it all started. I wasn't expecting any problems. But then last night when I go to meet the guy he turns out to be a white kid. Well, I didn't want to seem impolite. I couldn't tell him he was the wrong color. I mean, I could never say such a thing. To anyone. But the thing is the kid was wounded. He said his name was Billy but he might have just been making it up. I'll bet a lot of the boys don't tell me their real names. You know? But, anyway, I was sort of confused as to why Leon sent me a white kid this time, but also, it was so unsettling, he had this gash along the side of his head, above the ear, and his hair was matted with dried blood and what looked like burnt sand or something. And I asked him if he was all right and if he was sure he wanted to go through with this. He said yes, so I, you know, unzipped him and leaned over and tried to do it, but I couldn't get that picture of his bloody head out of my mind. I mean, I made sure that he got off, I always do, but I couldn't get hard. You know? So when it was over I wrote down the location of the nearest emergency room on the back of my business card and gave it to him. I mean, I offered to drive him there but he said no. He just got out of the car and I drove home. I swear. That was the last time I saw him. Then the next thing I know you guys are bashing down my office door accusing me of murder, embarrassing me in front of all my employees. But I didn't do it. Really. I'm not that kind of person. I would never hurt anyone. There. That's my story. For the fourth time. You guys are really something, you know? I mean I've got better things to do than sit around and keep you entertained. You know, I've been thinking. All the time I've been sitting here I've had time to think. And you know what? I figured something out. Because, to tell you the truth, Billy isn't the first boy I had an appointment with who wound up dead. There was another one. Tobias. I saw his picture in the paper. Said he was a crack addict allegedly killed by a dealer. Something like that. Anyway, I recognized him. And the name in the paper was the same one he gave me. Tobias. And you know what? He was black. But the cops never found the killer. Maybe they never even tried. Because he was black. The only reason you care about Billy is because he was white. Am I right? Maybe his parents are rich and famous or something. The papers will keep hounding you to find his killer. But nobody cared when the black kid got killed. You guys are really something. I'm not a criminal. I live in a nice house. Hell, you could call me a social worker. I provide poor youngsters with an income. You guys should be giving me a medal, not torturing me with all these stupid questions. Can I call my wife now?

[END DELETE]

THE JACK & THE KING

Diego stopped sucking Sammy's cock just long enough to say, "You've got quite a slab of meat there. Can I take home what I can't finish here?" He re-engulfed Sammy's thick rod and sucked it like a vacuum cleaner.

"I'm all out of doggie bags," said Sammy, grinning. "I guess you'll just have to eat it all now. There are people starving in Poland, you know."

Diego pulled away again. Took a long breath and said, "Speaking of poles, mine is getting hard and lonesome. Maybe you could pay it some attention?" He continued slurping while Sammy maneuvered his body, bringing them both face-to-cock. He pulled Diego's shaft into his mouth, circled his lips around it and slid them up and down. Ever so slowly.

Diego, the definitive stud, caressed Sammy's head between his massive thighs and fondled his dangling ballsac. Sammy responded by inserting his index finger into Diego's ass. He pushed it in as far as it could go, then gently drew it in and out. Diego sighed, quivered, then shook wildly and deposited a formidable load in Sammy's throat. As soon as Sammy tasted the salty cream, he favored Diego with a sample of his own succulent jism.

They rolled apart and waited for the spasms to subside.

Then Sammy—all lithe and wiry—changed position so the two men were lying head-to-head and toe-to-toe. They fell asleep and remained that way until the alarm clock rang out and awakened them two hours later.

*

They had met for the first time at the Backdoor bar earlier that evening. Diego, the coppery-skinned, pencil-mustached muscle-hunk had been shooting pool. Sammy, the well-defined, sinewy man with the unusually large endowment, had been leaning against the jukebox smoking a cigarette. Sammy had watched Diego bend over to score a double ricochet, and the bleached-out seam separating his meaty butt had beckoned to him like a long-lost friend. His cock began to squirm, growing larger by the second, as he imagined his throbbing rod exploring the cavern within. He'd bought another beer and strolled over to the green felt table. When the game had ended, Sammy locked his gaze on Diego's brown, puppyish eyes and smiled. Diego returned the gesture.

"Can I get you a beer or something?"

Diego glanced at Sammy's bulging crotch. "I know what I want, but I don't think it's on the menu."

"If you're as hungry as I am," said Sammy, "maybe we could find something good to eat at my place." He winked. Diego winked back and extended his hand.

"The name's Diego. Sometimes they call me the Jack of Diamonds."

Sammy grasped his hand in a firm clasp. "Sammy, also known as the King of Hearts."

"Not the broken ones, I hope."

"Not tonight," said Sammy.

They'd walked to Sammy's apartment through the balmy, starlit night, attempting to out-quip one another. But they seemed to be a pretty well-matched pair.

"I couldn't help but admire your back-seat upholstery," Sammy had said.

"It's difficult finding the right interior *dickorator* these days," Diego had countered.

Then, glancing at Sammy's tumescent crotch, Diego had said, "With artillery like yours, looks like you could win a war single-handed."

Sammy grinned. "With artillery like mine, I'm afraid it takes both hands!"

They'd chuckled and continued walking, until they'd arrived at Sammy's. Upon entering, he'd invited Diego to sit on his bed while he fiddled with his alarm clock.

"What are you doing?" Diego had asked.

"Setting the alarm. It'll go off every two hours. If we should fall asleep, it'll wake us up. This night's too good to waste. I can tell already."

They'd started out with a jack-off contest. On many previous occasions Sammy had challenged his guests to see who could shoot the most cum the farthest distance. But that night, with Diego, he wanted to have serial multiple orgasms, so the quantity was not nearly as important as the distance.

"How far do you think you can shoot your stuff?" Sammy had asked.

Diego looked at him and said, "So, you're a distance freak, eh?"

Sammy smiled and said, "Well, not to brag or anything, but once I was sitting right here on the bed and shot a load that landed on the far wall."

Diego estimated the distance. "Must be a good ten feet. You were in a sitting position?"

Sammy nodded. "Yeah. It would have been even farther if I'd been standing."

"I accept your challenge, champ."

Sammy fetched a roll of masking tape and laid a strip on the floor. Diego did a few deep-knee bends, as though warming up for the 50-yard dash. His thighs and calves tensed like an Olympic triathlete's.

They stood at the foul line with their toes almost touching it. Sammy scooped a handful of grease from the can and Diego followed suit. They wrapped their dangling cocks in their fists and greased them from base to tip. Stroking themselves—back and forth, up and down—their cocks began to lengthen and grow erect. Soon they were rocking to and fro, their cocks fucking their hands like the pistons of a super-charged engine.

Sweat broke out on Sammy's forehead and Diego grunted with each thrust of his pelvis. Faster and faster they stroked themselves until suddenly Diego let forth an arcing stream of jism that landed on the floor about seven and a half feet away. A few seconds later, Sammy shot his load and several dollops of cum sprang forth, hitting the floor just a few inches behind Diego's.

"I guess you win," said Sammy sheepishly.

"There's always next time," Diego grinned. "Come kiss the winner."

He pulled Sammy into a tight embrace, their cocks pressed up against their stomachs. Diego forced his tongue into Sammy's moist, warm mouth and pushed it to the back of his throat. Sammy had moaned with delight at that point and led Diego to the bed.

They'd followed that with blow jobs. The ingestion of pure protein would surely help them make the night an especially memorable one. Then they'd fallen asleep, recouping their strength, lightly dozing until the alarm clock summoned them back to consciousness and the possibility of more burning action.

*

Diego was facedown when the alarm sounded. His perfect buns—the size and shape of a halved basketball—looked as though they were desperately in need of some attention. When Sammy awoke, he couldn't help but notice the beckoning butt. His cock sprang to attention, standing up perpendicular to his abdomen. He greased his palm and moistened the throbbing shaft. It gleamed like a rocket, reflecting the light of the moon through the open window.

Sammy slid onto Diego's back. "Hey there, Superman," said the bottom, "you got a deposit for my savings account?

Interest is compounded hourly."

Sammy chuckled. "I hope there's no penalty for early withdrawal. The night's still young, you know."

Sammy's chest hovered over Diego's back and his cock poked at the entrance to Diego's tunnel of lust. The burning tip, already sticky with pre-cum, parted the opening and entered cautiously—like a coal miner exploring a promising vein of ore. As Sammy's burning rod inched its way closer to the father lode, Diego groaned with pleasure. His nipples hardened and his buns tensed, increasing the pressure on Sammy's cock. He sighed and rammed his way to glory. Diego's cock, stretching out between his belly and the sheet, sent waves of delight racing throughout his body, causing his breath to quicken. Sweat broke out on his forehead as he raised his ass in perfect rhythm to the downward thrust of Sammy's pelvis. Balls knocking against Diego's spread thighs, he raised and lowered himself as though doing push-ups. He could feel the pressure building in his groin. Flames of tension rose higher in his lower stomach and upper thighs. The moonlight illuminated Sammy's creamy white ass as it rose up and down, driving his Louisville Slugger to a grand slam. Diego's cock began to throb and he moaned. "Give it to me! Harder! Oh yeah!"

"Happy to oblige, tough guy. If you think you can take it."

"I'll take whatever you got and more," he gasped.

The rhythm sped up, the intensity grew almost unbearable. Suddenly Sammy yelled, "Thar he blows!" and huge gobs of cum shot through Diego's innards. Feeling the hot, molten lava spreading through his insides, he couldn't hold out any longer. His own cock smeared the sheet beneath him with pearly cream—the proof of a job well done.

After slowly pulling out and away, Sammy rolled off of Diego and lay panting by his side. Diego rolled over and glanced at him.

"That was pretty fuckin' fantastic," said Diego with a beaming smile.

"I've had lots of practice," Sammy smiled back.

"You can practice on me anytime."

"Shall I set the alarm again?"

"What are you waiting for?"

Sammy pressed the button and rolled onto his side. Diego wrapped his body around him—chest-to-back, cock-to-ass—and they tried to doze off as the earth slowly turned away from the moon.

*

Adrenalin was flowing, coursing through the circulatory systems of the Jack of Diamonds and the King of Hearts. Both had closed their eyes, but neither was capable of falling asleep at this point.

They lay there, pretending, until Sammy got up to pee. When he emerged from the bathroom, Diego did the same.

Staring at each other, they sat on the bed as the first rays of dawning light came through the open window, accompanying the soft breeze that felt so good on their naked skin.

Sammy glanced down at Diego's wilted cock, looked up and said, "My ass is feeling a bit neglected and I thought, perhaps, you would favor me with the touch of your jackhammer there."

Diego grinned. "I'm always happy to oblige a friend in need. You want to eat the pillow or put footprints on the ceiling?"

Without skipping a beat, Sammy replied, "The ceiling could use something to liven it up. Hasn't had a paint job in years."

Sammy rolled onto his back and threw his legs up over his head. Diego reached for the lubricant and lathered first his own cock and then Sammy's. He rubbed both cocks up and down—one in each hand—until they were as hard as granite.

Sammy watched Diego's sculpted torso hovering above him, an attractive sight at any time, but even more so in the pale light of morning.

Diego eased himself into Sammy's tight asshole. First Sammy groaned, then moaned and finally sighed once entry was complete. He grabbed his own cock and worked his clenched fist up and down the shaft from the tip to the base.

Diego began thrusting in and pulling out—not all the way, though—slowly increasing the speed and intensity. Eventually, the motion and impact was similar to that of a jackhammer, as requested. Sammy began raising and lowering his hips, following the pattern that Diego had established. Faster and faster, harder and harder, the motion intensified until Diego suddenly cried out, "Oh my God!" His body squirmed in uncontrollable spasms as he fired a load of sizzling cum into Sammy's eager ass. When Sammy felt the hot juice filling him up inside, he could hold back no longer. He squirted a stream of cum which looped into the air and settled in among the sparse hair on his handsomely chiseled chest.

"How was that?" Diego asked Sammy, grinning from ear to ear.

"Next time the city needs a street torn up, I'll recommend you," he smiled back.

"I'm pretty particular about how and where I use my tools."

"Good, I'd hate to think that you wasted your talents where they weren't appreciated."

Diego slowly pulled his still-hard dick from Sammy's firm butt. It made a slight popping sound as it cleared the entrance and flopped against his thigh.

"Do you think I should set the alarm again?" Sammy asked.

Diego looked at the clock. "Gee, I don't know. I have to be at work pretty soon."

"How about a shower?"

"Terrific idea."

They rose from the bed and moved to the bathroom. Sammy started the water, parted the shower curtain and they both stepped into the off-white porcelain tub.

Sammy picked up the bar of soap and stood away from the shower head as Diego doused his firm body in the pulsing waterfall. Working up a creamy lather, Sammy began soaping Diego's sexy contours. First the broad shoulders and powerful arms. Then the hard chest and—turning him around—the smooth back. His firm, meaty buns and strong, muscular thighs were saved for second to last. The stomach, shaft and balls served as a grand finale.

"Ouch!" Diego protested. "I guess I'm a little sore at this point."

"Me too," Sammy confessed. "But it was well worth it."

"Agreed."

Diego spun around beneath the falling water, rinsing the soap from his tingling body. Then he seized the soap and lathered up Sammy's taut chest, sinewy arms, hard stomach, huge cock and dangling balls. He turned him around and soaped up the prominent shoulder blades, the tapering lower back and the high white-as-snow buns. Then stooping, he cleaned the ropy-muscled legs and finally put the soap in the tray and watched Sammy rinse off.

They toweled themselves dry, got dressed and sat in Sammy's breakfast nook. He brewed strong Columbian coffee and prepared some eggs and toast. They ate in silence, bathing in the afterglow of sensuality that pervaded every inch of their bodies. The FM radio played some soft rock music in the background.

Then, when they were finished eating, they hugged and kissed. Sammy walked Diego to the door and opened it slowly. "Anytime you'd like to play again, I'll be ready, willing and able."

"I knew we'd eventually find something we could agree on."

SEDER

I sit at a large rectangular table in a huge Upper West Side apartment. There is a plate before me with a roasted lamb shankbone, a hard boiled egg, bitter herbs, charoses, karpas, glasses of salt water and goblets of wine. Also seated at this table is part of the family of my boyfriend, David, who sits beside me. I've never met anyone in his family before and I haven't been to a Passover seder in more than twenty years. I am slightly nervous. Partially because I'm in a roomful of strangers. Also, I don't even know why I'm here.

David's Uncle Harry is seated at the head of the table, this being his home. At the other end is his wife, David's Aunt Cel. The other places are occupied by various aunts, uncles and cousins. David's parents are absent, visiting relatives in Israel.

Harry begins to read from the Haggadah. "Blessed art though, O Lord our God—"

But suddenly Sol, sitting directly opposite from me says, "In Hebrew, Harry, please."

Harry stops reading and slowly looks up. He is a very large man, thick everywhere with a sprawling belly, a bushy mustache and big brown eyes. "Not everyone understands Hebrew," he says.

Sol, thin, darting eyes with a beak-like face, hands and arms always moving says, "I'm aware of that. But it's supposed to be in Hebrew!"

There is a bridge table a few feet away with four children, who for reasons I can't perceive, have begun yelling at one another. Judy, the young woman seated on my left is the mother of at least two of them, so she rises to quell the disturbance.

"He touched my matzoh," whines the blonde girl, Rachel. As Judy quiets them down, my attention returns to the argument at the adult's table.

"Hebrew!" says Sol.

"English," insists Harry. "This is America, not Israel."

"Hebrew," says Sol, with reverence, "out of respect for God."

"God?" says Harry, almost mocking. "What God? The one that slept through the Holocaust and is still, apparently, unavailable for comment?"

Sol mumbles something in Hebrew, then says, "If you don't believe in God why have a seder?"

Harry fixes him with a victorious stare and says, "Tradition!"

Barbara, Sol's wife, says, "Why don't we vote? Majority rules?"

David, sitting at my right, leans over to whisper in my ear. "We may be here all night and never get around to the food." I smile. His hand, under the table, behind the Indian madras tablecloth, squeezes my thigh then briefly clamps over my crotch bulge. I blush. Glance around to see if anyone has noticed David's action or my response.

Just then, Rhoda, David's cousin, strikes a pose like a comedienne and says, "What the fuck difference does it make?"

Barbara, her mother, scowls. "Watch your language!"

Rhoda, ignoring her, continues, sing-songy, "Hebrew, English, English, Hebrew. Words are words. Let's eat!" A very plump woman, she makes most of us laugh when she puffs up her cheeks and starts to shovel food toward her mouth, an invisible utensil and imaginary food.

Cel says, "Harry, why don't you read part of it in English. Sol, you can read the rest in Hebrew."

They begin to alternate paragraphs and I recall that David has instructed me not to bring up the subjects of religion, sex, or politics, so my game plan was to keep my thoughts to myself. But I'd asked, "If your family won't discuss religion, sex, and politics what will they talk about?"

"Oh, we'll discuss them all right. Just don't you be the one to bring them up. In fact," he'd added, grinning, "you just might want to stay on the sidelines and avoid the verbal daggers which will be flying like airborne latkes." He'd laughed. "I exaggerate. It's not that bad. We'll have fun. You'll see."

I was extremely agitated, my nerves like misfiring spark plugs as we entered the home of his Uncle Harry and Aunt Cel. She'd answered the door and David had said, "This is my Aunt Cel."

"Aunt Seal?" I'd said.

She'd laughed. A tall, slender woman with cascading black hair, she wore a yellow caftan with a turquoise and silver medallion. "Cel, short for Cecilia."

"Oh," I'd said, my face burning, probably fire engine red, wishing I could shrink to the size of a cockroach and scoot away.

She'd taken my hand, led me down the hall. "I was born Cecilia, called Celia through college and ever since I've been married it's just been Cel. Come, let me show you around."

It's an enormous place, my entire apartment could fit within the living room of this one. There is also a dining room, three bedrooms, a book-lined study and two bathrooms. A spectacular view of Riverside Park, the Hudson River and the Palisades, cross-ventilation in almost half the rooms.

In the dining room she pointed out the tablecloth from India, salt and pepper shakers from Nigeria, wine goblets from Switzerland. On the walls, folk art from Indonesia and South America. Harry and Cel travel a lot.

As we moved into the living room, David checked the Band-Aid on his neck which covers the only lesion on his body that is detectable when he's fully clothed. When I'd asked him if his family knew that he was HIV Positive, like myself, he shrugged and said he'd tell them when it became necessary to do so and not until. "Let's not get into a discussion about AIDS either," he'd amended his earlier instructions.

I was introduced to Rhoda, a squat woman in jeans and a long billowing shirt. And Mark, one of those extraordinarily handsome men with dark coloring, curly hair, sensitive but rugged face, hard and lean, the Mediterranean look—he could be from Spain, Italy, Greece or Israel. I thought David was attractive—trim body, earnest face, wild brown hair. But his cousin Mark is sensational. And Barbara, an aunt, wears a silk blouse, tourmaline, with a matching skirt, strands of lustrous pearls, huge gemstones on her fingers. Her hair, stiff and lacquered, looks like nothing could budge a single strand.

I'm never good at meeting a lot of strangers at one time. But I dutifully greeted uncles Harry and Sol, cousins Stuart and Judy, and a bunch of kids who ran from room to room, chasing, pinching, taunting, squealing.

We sip wine, dip parsley in salt water, then Harry breaks the matzoh and hides the afikoman. When he returns—I figure it's probably in the master bedroom—Sol mumbles something in Hebrew. We drink more wine. David snaps off a corner of matzoh and eats it. Stuart, husband of Judy, brother of Rhoda, son of Sol and Barbara—I'm finally getting the lineage—says, "You're not supposed to eat it yet."

David chews and swallows guiltily.

"How am I supposed to teach Judy and my children about Passover if you're going to break all the rules?"

Rhoda says, "Fuck the rules," and reaches for the matzoh.

"Watch your language," says Barbara.

I look briefly at Judy, a slim beauty with long blonde hair parted in the middle, then down at my plate.

I haven't had many Jewish boyfriends. It makes no difference to me. But this seems to be what David wants. Am I Jewish enough for him? Should I care? I haven't known him long enough to consider him anything more than a friend and fuck-buddy. A safe fuck buddy. I'm not sure if there's potential for more.

Stuart, somewhat dumpy-looking, with listless eyes and bad posture, says, "It's time for the Four Questions."

"Rachel's the youngest," says Sol.

"But she's not old enough to read yet," protests Judy.

"Jeremy will read them this year," says Harry, with grandfatherly pride.

The chestnut-haired boy—I imagine David looked like him at his age—stands, everyone looks toward the children's table and he begins to read, "Why is this night different from any other night?" His voice is soft and meek but he has no trouble with the words.

When I was born no one asked me if I wanted to be Jewish, if I desired any religious affiliation or would rather be without. I played the game for a while. It wasn't difficult. My family was not very religious. Assimilation was the goal. Now and then I was expected to be a good Jewish boy. But mostly, the all-American kid. Judaism offered a few pleasures but was never a way of life. Chanukah presents were nice, getting out of school for Yom Kippur added to the attraction, potato pancakes and stuffed derma made me proud. I can still remember the words to "Mi Y'Malel," and the way we puffed up our chests and sang from the heart in Sunday school, creating costumes for the Purim festival. But just as vividly I can hear the echoes of the words: kike, but you don't look Jewish; yid, but you don't act Jewish; Christ-killer; she's a typical JAP; he tried to overcharge me and I had to Jew him down; all Jews have a great sense of humor; she's got a big nose like a Jew.

These words used to jolt me like electric shocks, and they still do, to a lesser degree. These days I am witness to millions of slurs directed toward all kinds of people, coming from all kinds of people. I realize that everyone hates everybody. I hear black people bad-mouthing Koreans, Episcopalians putting down Catholics, the Kuwaitis don't like the Jordanians, the French despise the Germans, most of the world is unfair to women, mommies and daddies beat up their kids and everyone hates the queers.

We all sip wine.

Rhoda reaches for a matzoh but Barbara slaps her hand away.

We drink more wine.

A citizen of planet Earth is expected to swear allegiance to a religion, a race, a homeland, a doctrine, a role and at all times honor the traditional chains of opposition. But something inside me, my conscience perhaps, struggles against this, questioning, condemning. If being a Jew means accepting that the Arabs and the Germans are my natural enemies, that everytime an eye is plucked another must be plucked in return, then maybe I should search for something more civilized.

Jeremy completes his task and there is a sweet warmth in the room, as though some youthful effluence has permeated the air and intoxicated all of us. When he sits down and utters an audible sigh of relief, everyone smiles as Harry begins a call and response passage, the collective voices forthright and sincere. David goes for my crotch again. I reciprocate. We exchange conspiratorial expressions.

It's time for Sol to read about the plague. He carefully spills drops of wine while negotiating the intricacies of Hebrew articulation. Judy goes to the children's table and lists the plagues in English, softly, like a descant to Sol's oration. Blood. Frogs. Gnats. Flies. Murrain. Boils. Hail. Locusts. Darkness. Slaying of the First-Born.

"Kinda sounds like the next Stephen King novel," quips Rhoda.

I can't help laughing out loud. I stop myself, embarrassed.

Sol bangs both fists on the table, taking everyone by surprise. He turns to Rhoda. "Have some respect! Why do you torture me so?"

The atmosphere has vanished. As though a rush of cold air blew in from an open window.

"It was a joke, Dad, just a joke," she says apologetically. "I'm sorry."

She seems truly repentant. I sense that she didn't expect he'd react so severely, didn't intend to upset him.

"You're always sorry!" he snaps.

She leans back, her chest suddenly heaving, holds onto the edge of the table with whitening fingers splayed. The look of contrition, with eyes wide and mouth agape, turns into anger, her face tight. "When are you gonna give me a break, huh?" she shouts. "I can never please you!"

"Why did you come here tonight?" his face is crimson.

Barbara looks horrified, as though he might have a heart attack any second. "Stop it! Both of you!"

Sol continues. "Did you come here to honor your family and your religion, or just to get a free meal?"

I wince and look at Harry and Cel. They appear calm, as though this happens all the time.

"You'll never forgive me for being me. Right, Dad? Face it. I'm a lezzie, a queer, a bulldagger, a dyke."

With each of these words Sol recoils as though slapped.

Harry claps his hands. "Okay, enough. Unless you two care to take it outside."

"I think it's time to eat," says Cel, rising and moving toward the kitchen.

I overhear Judy whispering to the children, "Because sometimes Aunt Rhoda does things that your grandfather doesn't understand." She smooths Rachel's hair, pats Jeremy's head and returns to the adult's table.

I avoid looking at Sol. If he can't understand his daughter's sexual proclivities, what chance is there that he approves of me? Or David? I turn to look at him. He squeezes my thigh.

"Uncle Sol," he says, "you never criticize my, er, lifestyle. Why do you always give Rhoda such a hard time?"

I'm too embarrassed by this unflinching honesty to look at either Sol or Rhoda, so I stare at a painting on the wall.

He scowls. "It's different for women. They should have babies."

"There's no law that says that everyone in the world has to have children."

"She's my daughter!"

"Sol, Sol," pleads Barbara, desperate to calm him, change the subject.

I turn to Judy. "You must really be religious to know all the plagues by heart."

"I'm studying. To convert. I was raised Presbyterian. And when I married Stuart I decided I wanted to have a Jewish home for my children." She smiles, then whispers, "Do you think that if you and David decide to live together that you'll convert?"

"Me?" I say, stupefied. "I'm Jewish."

A look of disbelief moves across her face. "Oh, I thought..."

I pat her hand and smile to let her know that I'm not offended.

If the goons were to come right now and forcibly herd us all into concentration camps, which would I prefer, the Jewish one or the gay one? In the former there'd be no obvious consensus, only genetic connections and certain doctrines to which some would subscribe. Relationships would be arbitrary. Like at family gatherings. Where you talk to people once or twice a year and have only mundane subjects to discuss because you and your relatives share no interests, linked only by blood. And, anyway, how does one really define a Jew? Does my birth make it automatic? If I don't believe and don't practice, then, am I even eligible for the Jewish enclosure?

In the gay camp there'd be no question of my credentials. I could easily summon eyewitnesses and produce written and videotaped evidence that I am a bona fide homosexual being. And because there are people like me from every niche of human society, I think the chances of finding people with whom I have something to get thrilled about are much greater. I'd probably be a lot happier. Of course, there are Jews from all sectors of the globe as well. This is something I found out after spending my entire youth thinking that Jews only lived in New York and Israel. Since then I've met

Jews from Ireland, Texas and China. So I'd probably meet interesting people in both situations, but I'd most likely have more fun in the gay one. But there's also the possibility that I would be sent to a special camp for the HIV Positive. Anything can happen in America. My Japanese-American friends will readily attest.

David's cousin, Mark, the extraordinarily handsome one, hasn't said a word. He occasionally goes to the children's table and talks softly to them. He's probably the father of the other two kids, but where's the mother?

I'm suddenly overwhelmed by a coughing fit, something that I go through three or four times a day, a chronic post-nasal drip, a sign of my weakened immune system. I turn from the table, hacking, blowing my nose, wiping the tears from my cheeks. Cel asks, "Are you all right?"

Everyone looks at me with solicitude.

"Fine. Just my allergies," I lie, honoring David's request not to mention the plague that God didn't think of when the Israelites were in bondage.

Cel brings in platters and bowls and the clinking and tinging of forks, knives and serving spoons on plates begins.

Stuart asks David how long he and I have been together.

David looks at me. "About three months?"

I nod.

"How did you meet?" asks Rhoda, leering.

"Well," says David, "we were at a—wait, you tell it," he turns to me.

I'd just forked some very tasty pot roast into my mouth and I have to finish chewing. I put down my fork and look up. Everyone is staring at me with—I'm not sure exactly, curiosity, interest—I feel like a klieg light is shining on me and ten million strangers are about to solemnly judge my every word.

"We were at a peace rally," I say cautiously, unaware of the ratio of hawks to doves.

David says, "Yeah, it was just like the sixties!"

I nod. "We were both with the ACT UP contingent and we introduced ourselves and started talking and then went for coffee afterwards. Eventually we started dating."

Rhoda winces and says, "Dating! Ugh!"

"Nothing terribly exciting," I add, "movies, plays, dinner."

"And a few other things, I'll bet," says Rhoda.

Everyone chuckles as I pick up my fork and resume eating, hoping that this line of conversation is over, that someone will jump into the void of silence which now wafts into the room like a fine mist.

"Peace rally!" says Sol. "I think we should have gone further. I'm with Schwartzkopf."

"*Dumkopf*, you mean," says Stuart.

Sol wipes his chin and places the napkin in his lap with dramatic deliberation. "I'll have none of your anti-Americanisms. Not now. Not on Passover."

"I don't want my children to grow up in a world full of violence and hatred," says Stuart.

"He's right, Sol," says Harry. "War begets fear which begets hate which begets war."

"Cock 'n' bull!" says Sol, starting to eat again, a fierce though distant look on his face which suggests he has dropped out of the conversation and intends to ignore everyone.

We continue eating.

David's relatives share certain traits and propensities with my aunts, uncles and cousins. And coincidentally, one of my cousins also married a gentile, except that ours has no plans to convert. However, the tension between Sol and Harry is just like that of my uncles on my mother's side, Harvey and Jacob, and the conflicts between Sol and Rhoda, very similar to my cousins Miriam and Jeffrey who engage in a perpetual one-upmanship contest about who has the tougher job and who earns the most money. But no one in my family knows I'm gay, and I don't think there are any others, with the possible exception of my cousin Laura who was very tomboyish when young and has been independent and single throughout her adult life. I imagine if David came to a family gathering of mine he would probably be as shocked and amused as I am.

David touches the Band-Aid on his neck and the distraction of seeing his hand rise, a blur of flesh from the periphery of my vision, pulls me back to the table.

"I cut myself shaving," he says to no one in particular.

Almost everyone has finished eating. I ingest one more forkful, pat my lips and tell Cel how much I enjoyed everything. I rise to help clear the table but Harry insists I sit. As the children go to search for the afikoman, fruit, coffee, tea and sponge cake are served. The wine and food have slowed everyone down. There is a lassitude hovering about the table.

It takes Rachel about two minutes to find the hidden matzoh. She triumphantly presents it to Harry who reaches into his pocket and gives her a dollar bill. He dandles her on his knees as the other children sulk at their table. Sol stands up, approaches them, slips them each a dollar instructing them not to tell Rachel, who is distracted by Harry. I gather this was pre-planned.

David clasps my thigh. Leans over and whispers, "I've had enough. You?"

I nod.

"Let's boogie."

As we say our goodbyes I shake hands with all the men, the women kiss my cheek. They all indicate that they hope to see me again soon. I feel like telling them the chances of David and I still being together by next Passover are pretty unlikely. There's our precarious health, of course. And I've never sustained any romantic or sexual relationships beyond a year. I'm not even certain why I came here tonight. I usually avoid contact with my friends' families. I don't know why I accepted this invitation. Perhaps I'm more involved than I suspected.

David and I walk down Broadway.

"You done good, kid," he says. "They loved you."

"I liked them. A lot. They reminded me of my own family, which I can only appreciate from a distance."

"Yeah, I know what you mean." He places his arm around my back. "Maybe we can do this again next year?"

"Sure," I say, not wanting to sound too pessimistic, unwilling to spoil the mood.

Suddenly David stops. I turn to see what's wrong. He tears the Band-Aid from his neck and tosses it into the gutter.

THE GARDEN OF TERRA IX

It was on a warm and sunny afternoon, just a few weeks after the farmers had begun their work, that Mark came running to the planting field. Breathless and agitated, he approached Tony and Liz who were talking beneath the shade of a tree just a few meters from the garden.

"The Captain asked me to organize a meeting for tonight," said Mark, trying to catch his breath. "Attendance by everyone is mandatory."

"Oh?" said Liz nonchalantly. "What's up?"

"Yeah," said Tony, "did they fix the communicom or something?"

"No," said Mark, shaking his head. "I'm not absolutely certain but I think he's going to discuss...compulsory procreation."

"Compulsory procreation?" queried Tony. He looked at Liz. She looked at him, then at Mark.

"You mean..." she said.

"Yes. We've got to start making babies."

"Making babies!" said Tony. "Why?"

"To keep the continuity of our community going," said Mark, "until we can escape or someone comes to rescue us."

"Sounds pretty intense to me," said Liz.

"I don't know if I can handle it," said Tony.

"Same here," she rejoined.

"If the Captain orders us to, then we have to," said Mark.

"Wow," said Liz. She shook her head. "I knew things might get rough on this planet, but I never imagined anything so...repulsive."

Tony and Mark nodded in agreement.

*

Like all of the others, Liz and Jana's hut had been constructed mostly of whatever could be salvaged from the wrecked Wayfarer. Many consisted of panels loosened from the hull, a chair or two from the recreation center and a thatched roof of twigs, vines and broad leaves. The crew members who were unattached ate and slept communally; couples had private domiciles. Liz and Jana sipped some tea and talked long into the night, past their usual bedtime.

"It could have been a lot worse," said Jana. "We could have crashed into a planet with no terraforming and we'd all be dead by now."

Liz sighed. "You're right. But still..."

"I know it seems awful but we've all gotta do it. Look at it as an unpleasant but necessary task that you only have to do once and then never again."

Liz put her cup on the flat stone that served as a table. "That's easy for you to say, you've done it with men before. I thought I'd never have to."

Jana crossed her legs and straightened her spine. "That's true. I guess you might say I'm experienced a little." She grinned. Then her expression became serious. "But I find the prospect just as repugnant as you do."

"Is it as awful as I imagine it is?"

Jana snickered. "Well, there's a reason why I fell in love with you. What we do is more fun. But still—to be fair—I'd have to say that it varies from man to man. Some are more considerate than others. Or less obnoxious, as the case may be."

"I hope I get a pleasant one," said Liz with resignation.

"I hope we both get pleasant ones," said Jana. She moved

alongside of Liz and draped her arm over her shoulder. "You'll see, it won't be that bad. I'm dreading the pregnancy more than the body contact."

"I hadn't even thought about that part," said Liz. "Nine months of sheer agony."

"Not to mention the delivery."

"Yeah," said Liz, "the delivery." She grimaced.

"Let's not worry about it until we have to," said Jana, kissing her cheek. "We should try to get some sleep."

They undressed and extinguished the candle. Then lay in each other's arms on the pallet they'd built just inside the doorway of the small hut.

*

The blue sun was setting over the treetops as Tony and Mark strolled through the woods before dinner. It was Tony's turn to cook and he always avoided it for as long as possible. Mark had gotten used to this and always snacked on wild berries to forestall his hunger. A squirrel scampered up a treetrunk and Mark said, "It's just like Earth here. Amazing."

Tony looked at him sharply. "On Earth men don't have to have sex with women if they don't want to," he said, making no attempt to conceal his anger.

"Look at it this way," said Mark. "At least you don't have to bear the child."

Tony sat on a log and picked up a stick. He poked it through the damp leaves that covered the floor of the forest. "A truism," he said. "And raising the kid might not be so bad."

"Sure," said Mark. "It'll be fun. You and I can still live together and the kids can spend half the time with us."

Tony looked at him incredulously. "You mean, you won't mind being a daddy? I thought you hated children!"

Mark shook his head. "I don't hate them. I just felt that I wasn't qualified to raise them. It sort of scares me...all that responsibility."

The sun was invisible now. A violet glow along the horizon

was all that remained. The forest was a labyrinth of shadows.

"How are they gonna decide who breeds with who?" Tony asked.

"Good question. Hadn't thought of that. But I'm sure Captain Shepherd and Officer Harker have something in mind."

"When do you think we'll find out?"

"Soon. Probably."

Tony asked, "Getting hungry?"

"To tell the truth, yeah. You?"

He nodded. "Might as well face the inevitable and fix us something to eat," said Tony, rising, tossing the stick into the shadows.

"Might as well," agreed Mark and followed him back toward their hut near the beach.

*

The garden was beginning to show the effort that had been put into it. There were small green tomatoes, young ears of corn and tiny orange petals on the marigold shoots. Tony and Liz had been working all morning and hadn't said a word to each other.

"I guess we're going to have to talk about this sometime," said Liz, breaking the heavy silence. She looked over at Tony who'd stood up, brushing dirt from his knees.

"Talk about what?" he said diffidently.

"Us," she said. "And our baby."

"What's there to talk about? Just tell me where and when and I'll do my best," he snapped.

Liz threw down her makeshift hoe and strode over to him. "Look," she said, "I'm not any happier about this than you are. But the least we can try to do is make it pleasant for each other. This wasn't my idea, you know."

Their eyes met. "I'm sorry," he said. "You're right."

They sat in the shade of a tall tree. A gentle breeze ruffled their hair as a rabbit poked its head through the tall grass then disappeared.

"You know what's really bothering me?"

"No," she said. "Tell me."

"I'm prepared to deal with the kid and all. I'll try to be a good father. It's just that..."

"What? I can be very understanding."

"It's just that I don't know if we're supposed to...make love or just do it fast and get it over with." His face flushed crimson and he looked away.

Liz smiled. "Any way you want. Just be easy with me," she said.

"You go easy with me, too," he said.

"We'll make this as easy for each other as we can," she said, taking his hand in hers. They smiled at one another. Then went back to work.

*

The reflection of the red sun rippled like a soft, flat disc on the surface of the ocean. It was late afternoon, on a small stretch of sand far away from the remains of the spacecraft, where Liz took off her shirt as Tony removed his shorts. She looked at him nervously. Then turned around to finish undressing. Tony took off his undersling and stood there, not knowing what to do next. Liz turned and looked down at the blanket on the sand.

"Maybe we should lie, I mean sit down," she said. Tony nodded. They knelt.

Tony inched toward her. "Well, here we are," he said.

Liz moved closer to him. He placed his arm around her neck. She turned her face toward him. Eyes closed, lips parted. He watched her face move closer, then closed his eyes and aimed his mouth at her lips. He lipped her nose as her mouth grazed his chin. She giggled. He laughed. They looked at each other and shook in spasms, slapping their thighs.

When she finally got herself under control, Liz said, "Maybe we should skip the romantic foreplay and get it over with."

"Good idea," he said, grinning.

She lay back and closed her eyes. He mounted her and closed his eyes. With a little cooperation and some tactful suggestions, they were able to accomplish what they'd set out to do.

*

Jana was cleaning the area in front of the hut. She scooped up a handful of dried brown leaves and placed them in a small basket she'd constructed of bark and vines. A yawning sound emanated from inside of the hut and moments later Liz came to the doorway. Shielding her eyes from the sun, she looked over at Jana. "I've been sleeping more," she said, then smiled and walked over to where Jana stood. She kissed her. They hugged.

"How do you feel?" Jana asked.

"I feel marvelous. Like there's been a chemical change in my whole body. I feel charged with life; alive and glad of it."

"Good," said Jana. She placed her hands on her own stomach and said, "It gets more intense. I know exactly how you feel. That's how I felt the first few weeks. It's grand, isn't it?"

"Yes," said Liz, beaming.

"Am I showing yet?" Jana swiveled to accentuate her profile.

"Not yet. But you look wonderful."

They stood there for a few minutes, looking at each other. The ocean, almost indigo at that hour, made kissing sounds on the shore.

"Let's lie together for a while," said Jana and led her into the hut. They lowered themselves to the pallet and held each other close.

*

They were in the forest, sitting on their favorite log in their chosen glade. Tony was breaking a stick into tiny slivers. Mark gazed at a painted bunting perched on the branch of a mulberry tree.

"You seem awfully nervous," said Mark.

"I'm just wondering about stuff."

"What kind of stuff?"

Tony sighed. "You know. About the kid."

"What about the kid?"

"Well, you know. If it'll be normal, if it'll be a boy or a girl."

Mark nodded. "Yeah. I'm worried about my kid's health too. So's Laura. But who cares if it's a boy or a girl?"

"I care. And I'm also wondering if it'll be…"

"Be what?" Mark asked.

Tony inhaled deeply and his chest expanded. "If it's a straight girl or a lesbian or a gay boy I can handle it. But if it's a straight boy—oh gosh—I won't be able to teach him how to chase girls or any of that stuff."

"You know," said Mark, taking his hand, "that's what I was always afraid of. But now I realize that's not what's important. You teach the kid what you can and he or she will learn the rest elsewhere."

Tony's face registered surprise. "I never thought of it that way. You're right, though. I'll just explain moral stuff like right and wrong and teach educational stuff like who Gertrude Stein, Tennessee Williams, Billie Holiday and Stephen Sondheim were and stuff like that."

"Right," said Mark. "This might even be fun."

"It's gonna be great," said Tony. "We'll be daddies together and I'll be an uncle to your kid and you'll be an uncle to mine."

Mark smiled. They kissed. Then embraced. A few stars began to flicker in the twilit purple sky.

Other Books From BANNED BOOKS
(ISBN prefix: 0-934411)

Faultlines,
Stan Leventhal, $8.95, 26-3
A Herd of Tiny Elephants,
Stan Leventhal, $8.95, 13-1
Understanding Homosexuality: The Pride and the Prejudice (nonfiction),
Roger Biery, (hardback) $23.95, 37-9; paperback $15.95, 38-7
Syphilis As AIDS (nonfiction),
Robert Ben Mitchell, $8.95, 35-2
Death With Dignity,
Jack Ricardo, $8.95, 34-4
Alternate Casts,
Marsh Cassady, $8.95, 33-6
Silverwolf,
Roger Edmonson, $8.95, 32-8
Gay Tales & Verses Arabian Nights,
edited by *Henry M. Christman*, $7.95, 27-1
Fine Lines,
Gerard Curry, $7.95, 23-9
Two Novellas: Walking Water & After All This
Thom Nickels, $8.95, 22-0
Common Sons,
Ronald Donaghe, $8.95, 21-2
Sacred Cows,
Jed A. Bryan, $8.95, 20-4
gay(s)language,
H. Max, $4.95, 15-8
Like Coming Home: Coming-Out Letters (nonfiction),
edited by *Meg Umans*, $7.95, 12-3
Mountain Climbing in Sheridan Square,
Stan Leventhal, $8.95, 08-5
Kite Music,
Gary Shellhart, $8.95, 07-7
A Cry in the Desert,
Jed A. Bryan, $9.95, 04-2
Tangled Sheets,
Gerard Curry, $7.95, 02-6
FAIRY TALES Mother Never Told You,
Benjamin Eakin, $7.95, 00-X

Available from your favorite bookseller
or by mail from: BANNED BOOKS
#292, P.O. Box 33280, Austin, TX 78764

Add $1.50 postage and handling.
Send postage stamp for complete catalog.